SYSTEMA PARADOXA

ACCOUNTS OF CRYTOZOOLOGICAL IMPORT

VOLUME 01
WHEN THE MOON SHINES
A TALE OF THE SNALLYGASTERS

AS ACCOUNTED BY JOHN L. FRENCH

NEOPARADOXA
Pennsville, NJ
2020

PUBLISHED BY
NeoParadoxa
A division of eSpec Books
PO Box 242
Pennsville, NJ 08070
www.especbooks.com

ISBN: 978-1-949691-49-8
ISBN (ebook): 978-1-949691-48-1

Interior Design: Danielle McPhail
www.sidhenadaire.com

Cover Art: Jason Whitley
Cover Design: Mike and Danielle McPhail, McP Digital Graphics
Interior Illustration: Jason Whitley

Copyediting: Greg Schauer

DEDICATION

TO JACOB RUDOLPH

PROLOGUE

They had been asleep for several years. Resting, renewing their strength, living off the fat they had stored prior to their slumber. But now it was their time. Their bodies stirred, their hearts beat faster, and their blood warmed. Soon, they began to awaken.

Kona woke first, looking about, smelling the air, listening to the sounds of the woods. She sensed danger, there was always danger, but others could not get close to the place they had chosen for their nest, not like the cave.

The cave. She remembered the sorrow of the cave, and if she could have, she would have wept. But weeping was not in her nature. The past was a painful memory, but the present was all that now mattered.

Kona wanted to cry out, to announce to the forest creatures that their queen had awakened, but it was not yet time. *He* must awaken, then they must feed to restore their strength.

A low whistle sounded, one heard only by her. Forra was stirring, his blood warming. Soon his eyes would open. He would see her, and the bond between them would be renewed.

Forra's eyes opened, and he gazed into hers. Both felt the warmth that was not caused by blood. A yearning for each other that could not yet be satisfied as neither had the strength.

He raised his head, looked around at the place they had chosen. It was good. Clear ground, high up, difficult to approach unseen. Not like the cave.

The cave had been well hidden to the eyes of men and common beasts, but not to the hairy ones. They had sniffed and felt them out. When the chicks arrived but before they could fly, when Forra was out hunting, the hairy ones came.

The cave was narrow, and there was no escape from the back. Two by two, they attacked, trying to get past her, trying for the hatchlings. Kona fought. Lacking the room to use her wings or tentacles, she ripped at them with her sharp, shiny beak. She killed some, but others came and kept coming. She fought for their lives, a fight she could not win, not with the numbers against her. Her hatchlings — one like Forra, two like her — would be devoured, as would she.

Knowing that her death would not save her offspring, and with the cold reasoning of her kind, she fought her way through, killing more of the hairy ones but taking injuries from claw and tooth, wounds that would take a long sleep to heal. Once free of the cave, she lifted into the sky to escape the overwhelming pack. As she fled, her children called to her. Their young minds reached out to hers with desperate pleas for help. Their cries pierced her heart, but Kona could not save them. She could only avenge them.

When Forra felt her mind seeking him, when he saw her flying toward him, he knew that the cave and the young had been lost. Kona would not have left them otherwise. Their eyes met as they felt their bond, but this was not a time for the dance and the embrace. Together they flew from the cave, hunting the hairy ones. They caught three in a clearing, old ones that could not keep up with the pack. They would do.

Swooping down, she lifted one in her claws. She did not feed on it, did not pull the blood from its body, for it had fed on her offspring, and she did not want to taste her own.

The others Forra destroyed. One he tore apart with his teeth. The other he carried high as he searched for the pack. Once he found it, he dropped the corpse in their midst.

Their vengeance, such as it was, would not bring their offspring back. But it did show the hairy ones the cost of their attack.

Abandoning the cave, they flew south and, after a search, found the high ground. Landing, they searched by scent, sight, and mind. Not finding any trace of the hairy ones, they hunted and ate until they were *more than full. Then it was time for the sleep. Their wings folded, Kona's tentacles holding Forra close to her, they used their minds to fade away, to become part of the landscape, a part that would be ignored by anyone who came upon them. Only then did they sleep.*

The pack was starving. They were too great in number, and there was not enough prey. There were fights, and leadership changed many times.

To survive, they dared to attack the nest of the flying ones. The female fled, leaving her small ones. The three strongest of the pack had feasted on these. The ones that did found their minds strengthened, their senses heightened, their power to freeze and compel prey increased.

They should have fought, should have battled each other until two submitted. But their minds connected, and they joined their thoughts. As one, they directed the pack in the hunt.

No leader could bring food that was not there. In desperation, they led the pack away from the shadows and darkness that was their home and into the open ground to prey upon placid beasts as they grazed and slept. But then came their protectors, men with the power of thunder and pain. The pack was driven away; some were hurt, some left the pack forever. One of the three that lead them surrendered his essence to the earth.

Knowing there was only one path to survival, the pack split, some of its members following one leader north, some following the other south, back to where their kind had come, but where they had not been for many seasons.

In the light of the fat Moon, Kona and Forra left their nesting place and soared through the sky. They saw foxes and rabbits and once chased an owl from the sky, from their sky. Later they would share it with other raptors, but that night it was theirs alone.

Foxes and rabbits were too small to feast on that night. So they flew low, sending the prey their thoughts, awakening them, and sending them running in fright. Forra chased a doe out of hiding and into the open. Kona swooped and grabbed it in her talons.

She did not take it home. Instead, she flew high and fastened her tentacles around it. In the air, she drained it dry, then let its bloodless body fall to the ground. Forra saw cattle sleeping in their pen. They were restless, nervous, knowing something was not right, but unaware of what it might be. He too swooped. Using both claws, he lifted one of the beasts and flew it back to their high ground where he let his mate drink her fill before his razor-sharp teeth ripped the carcass apart so he could devour its meat.

Having fed well, Forra and Kona launched themselves into the sky as one. Once aloft, they became one in fact, her tentacles wrapping around him, taking pleasure from him and returning it to him. Rejoicing in their awakening, in their meal, and in each other, they cried out their delight, announcing their presence to all.

The pack had been in the woods for a half cycle of the Moon. To the other dwellers of the forest, the ones with instinct but no inherited memory, easy prey upon which the pack would grow fat, they were death on two legs.

More creatures came, creatures that walked like pack but moved like prey. They spoke loudly and made their way without caution so that all knew of their presence. Pack memory called the creatures "Man." Night after night, the pack watched them from the darkness but took no action. Man knew of the pack but had not seen them for many, many seasons. They were legend and myth, cautionary tales to frighten Man's young into obedience.

Verr, the pack leader, recalled that Man possessed the power of thunder and pain. They also called light to their command. Light that burned bright and hurt the pack's eyes. *Still*, Verr thought, *they are in our territory and have marked it, and this cannot be.*

We will attack them, kill them, devour them, Verr thought to his pack. *When you charge, close your eyes and be guided by their scent. Feast well.*

CHAPTER ONE

The night was still and bright with the light of a gibbous moon. Raphael Meadows was deep within the woods, watching over his still with the help of his sons. The still was not really his; it belonged to his clan. Not The Klan, mind you, Meadows would have no truck with that hooded group of crazies, but just his clan, a loose group of 'shiners related to each other in some way—brothers and sisters, cousins by birth or marriage, sometimes just folk from the same town back in the old country. Meadows's mother had been a Daly, and when he was just twelve, her brother took him out to his very spot to show him how to make what some call the pure, and others the stuff or the craythur, but mostly 'round these parts, it was just 'Shine.

It took more than just setting up the still, adding the ingredients, lighting the fire, and letting nature take its course. You had to make sure to get the proof right—some folks liked it mild and others strong, and there were some who felt that if the first sip didn't knock them on their ass, they hadn't gotten their money's worth.

And you had to be sure not to mix up poison. One jug of jake that left people paralyzed, blind, or dead was not only bad for business, it might lead you to be staked to the ground by your still, cut open with your guts spilled out, and left to feed the night's creatures. And don't expect any help from your clan. For what you did, for how you disgraced the family, they'll be the ones carrying the stakes and ropes and handing your knife to the victims' families to finish the job.

There was no cooking that night, just watching and guarding. It used to be your clan had its territory and two or three spots, just as other clans had theirs. You kept yourself to yourself, and if you had to crossover, you let them know you were coming, and you kept your gun broke open and your pistol, if you had one, out of sight. And you brought a bottle of your stuff in case you came across a site, and you shared with them and they shared with you and you each told the other how good theirs was, and you didn't dare look too long at how their still was fashioned, even if they let you get that close.

But if you came without warning, if you came sneaking or spying and you got caught, well, that's what shotguns were for, and all anyone would say at your wake was, "Damn fool had it coming. What in the hell was he thinking?"

But that was then, back when it was a more or less friendly competition among like-minded folk, where arguments were settled with fists and their resolutions celebrated with the pure.

But things change. The Government made that stupid-assed law about liquor and drinking, and what had been a family business was turning into big business with strangers moving in, trying to organize, and smashing the stills of those who won't go along.

"Think they'll be trouble, Da?" his son Thomas asked.

Meadows shook his head. "Probably not this far back. That's why we moved so they won't find us."

"Might be best to go along," suggested his younger son Sean. "Sell to them and let them sell to others."

Meadows thought for a moment. "It'll probably come to that. But the family will decide what's best. 'Til then, we stand our turn at watch and deal with any intruders." He checked his gun, made sure there were shells in its chambers. "You boys okay with that?"

It was a hard thing Meadows asked his boys, just fifteen and seventeen, to do. They'd used guns before, but on game, not men. Still, a boy had to grow up sometime, and part of that was protecting what was yours.

Thomas's "Yes, Da," was slow in coming. Sean's eager "Let them come. They won't leave," scared Meadows more than a little.

Pray God they don't come, Meadows thought to himself. He'd like it if his sons stayed boys for a little while longer. And he'd like it more if they lived to be men.

An hour went by, then another. Guns near at hand, Sean and Thomas took turns sleeping, Not Meadows, though. He'd sleep in the morning, but maybe not right away if the wife were willing. And if not, well, just the thought of his sweet Mary was enough to keep him awake.

They were three hours into their watch. Thomas heard it first, a low sound like a train whistle.

"Something about that sound," the boy said, "makes you think about going places and seeing things."

"Only thing is," Meadows said, "that whistle is getting louder. Far away as the tracks are, it shouldn't. And no trains run at night, not around here. Wake your brother."

Thomas shook Sean, who right away reached for his gun. "Is it them? Is it time?"

"Easy, Sean. I want you boys to check and make sure the hex signs are hanging in place in the trees, that's all. Sean, you take the light. Thomas, you guard your brother."

"Why, Da?"

"Just do it," Meadows said, a bit harsher than he meant to. "Just...do...it, and quickly. And if you see or hear...anything ...just hurry back to the light."

The boys went off, leaving Meadows alone and worrying. In his mind, he heard the sound of wings beating the air, the cawing of one for its mate. Was it the male with its sharp teeth that ripped and ate, or the female with the tentacles that could suck a man dry? He hoped and prayed that it was just his imagination, that there had been a train and the stillness of the night had carried its sound all this way. He prayed that those Amish were right about the — what was it that preacher had called them — heptagrams. Being a symbol of the Lord's proper creation, the hex signs should protect them against the improper beasts. But Meadows knew that "should" and "would" hardly ever meet in the backwoods.

The boys came back. "Everything's in place, Da," Thomas said. He was scared but calm, just as he should be. Gun in hand, Sean searched the shadows, looking for something that moved, something he could shoot.

Maybe I shouldn't bring that boy with me anymore. The way he is, he's apt to shoot himself or one of us.

As Meadows finished this thought, shadows moved in the moonlight. "Boys, stand ready," he called to his sons. "Don't shoot unless you must," he said, more to Sean than Thomas.

The fire backlights us, makes us easy targets, he thought, and considered dowsing it. But he knew the woods held more dangers than men, and if these were men on the hunt, he and his sons would by now be dead or dodging shot and slugs. "Throw on more wood," he ordered, hoping he was right even as he prayed he was wrong.

The shadows came closer. Meadows heard growling, and by the moon's light, he saw the beasts. To call them wolves would be to shame those noble beasts. These hairy creatures were larger, from the size of a calf to that of a bear. And no wolf ever walked on two legs.

Remembering the old tales and knowing what they faced, Meadows thought, *Dwayyo...the hex doesn't work on these*. But as the fire blazed up and the nearest back away, he remembered they didn't like the light. "More wood," he shouted.

From the corner of his eye, he saw his youngest raise his gun. "Sean, wait for them to come to us. And if they do, don't look them in the eyes."

In his mind, Meadows felt the pack, or thought he did. They were getting ready to charge, and they wanted him to know, wanted him frozen in fear. The hell with that. They might take him and his boys, but it would be at a cost.

The growling grew louder and came in unison, as if the pack were one. "Run while you can, boys, I'll hold them off." It was a slim hope but his only one.

"No, sir, we're with you."

"What Sean said, Da."

"I love you, boys."

"And we lov…"

And from deeper in the woods, the sounds of train whistles rose again as something with wings briefly eclipsed the moon. As if one being, the pack let out a great howl and ran after the noise.

The three men, for after bravely standing against death, Sean and Thomas were certainly no longer boys, waited to learn if they were indeed safe, waited until the whistles and growls met and they heard the sounds of a battle between them. Only then did the 'shiners relax.

"Never," Meadows said to his sons, "never in all my days did I expect a snally to save me from the dway." But as happy as he was to be alive, he knew that the dark creatures of the woods had awakened.

"I think it's time, boys, for the clan to talk to these strangers come to town and see about going to work for them. I think I'm done cooking 'shine."

As the pack was about to charge, a shadow passed over the Moon, and there came a sound that cut deep into their minds. The flying ones had awakened. Even if Verr had wanted to stop them, the pack could not resist the challenge from the sky, the claim that their territory did not belong to them. Leaving the men to be hunted another day, the dwayyo rushed toward their longtime foe.

The hairy ones hunt in these woods and are coming, Forra sent to his mate.

Kona, remembering the loss of her children, sent back, *Let them come. We are now together, in the open, not trapped in a cave.*

So as the dwayyo came for them, the snallygasters landed on the high ground and awaited them.

The flying ones are above us, Verr told the pack.

Rush them, hurt them, destroy them, devour them, the pack sent back, maddened by the scent of their foe.

Too late, Verr sensed the danger. These were not prey frozen by fear and thought to await slaughter. Running in front of the pack, he grabbed them, pushed them, snarled and growled at them to get back, to withdraw, to fight this battle at another time in a better place. But the pack would not be denied and charged the hill.

Again, the snallygasters took flight, this time dropping down on the dwayyo. Each of them picked up one in their claws. If they had not already fed that night, they would have devoured the helpless dwayyo in full view of their pack. But with their stomachs full, they simply flew high and dropped the trespassers from a great height, allowing their bodies to smash against the ground.

Seeing and feeling their own leaving the pack broke the spirit of the dwayyo. Turning, they retreated into the woods to return to their packhome. Verr was the last to leave. Watching as the two figures hovered above him, ready to slash out with his claws should they attack, he slowly backed away.

Remain on your high ground, Verr dared to send. *Do not come into our territory. If you do, you will be our meat.*

We grant you the place where you sleep and hunt, Kona and Forra sent back. *Do not come near our place again. Any that do will be taken from your pack.*

Challenges and warning having been made on both sides, the Snallygasters returned to their nesting site. The dwayyo leader followed his pack home, knowing what must be done. His pack had disobeyed him that night. There can only be one leader.

CHAPTER TWO

There was trouble when the gangs first moved in with their plans for roadhouses where people could get a decent drink at an honest price. Raphael Meadows knew there would be. The clans were a stubborn lot and did not take to strangers or change, especially when it cut into their 'shine business. There were strong objections, and there might have been gunfire and bloodshed on all sides. But then came the growls and the howls and the whistles in the woods.

"They're back," Meadows told the clan members when they met to decide what to do about the gangs. "The snallygasters and the dwayyo. Me and my boys heard the dway and saw their shadows. If they hadn't gone after the snallys, someone else would be talking right now."

Others had seen them as well or knew of someone who had gone into the deep woods and not returned. After some discussion, the clans decided that sometimes change was good and to leave the woods to the things that dwelt in its darkness and shadows.

The 'shiners and their family gave up the craft and went to work for the gangs. It was safer, mostly, and the money was good, better and easier than selling and making it on your own. The Italians were okay, the ones who came down from Chicago, but the Irish understood the way of things better, coming from the same county and sharing the same troubles and history. But both expected the same things—loyalty, obedience, and silence.

"This is how it's going to be," Patrick Burke told each man who came to work for him, "You keep your damned mouth shut about what you do, where you do it, and who you do it for. If you can't do that, now's the time to get out. If you stay in and flap your gums to the wrong person, then one day somebody's gonna take you for a walk in the woods and come back alone."

Vincent Sala said much the same thing to the men he hired for his roadhouses. "My people call it '*omerta*,' and it is a code to be followed. Tell no one your business and, more importantly, tell no one my business should you chance to learn of it. If you are given a task, do not speak of it even to your fellow worker. He does not need to know, and your task may involve him." Sala paused to let his words sink in. "Now some of you may be asking, 'What is the worst that could happen if I talk when I should not?' That is something you do not want to discover. But I can tell you that your loved ones will weep at your funeral, or you will weep at theirs."

Raphael Meadows went to work for Burke, doing what was needed but mostly bossing the men making cider, gin, and, of course, hard 'shine. Burke owned the roadhouse just outside of Bixby on the Coast City Pike. He had come down from Harbor City and had moved into a nice house in town. It was commonly believed that he had the backing of one of the crime lords that ruled that city.

"Charley Healy came by today," Meadows told Burke when the man came in to check on things. The two were at a table. It was early in the day, but the cider needed tasting. They both took long sips and pronounced it good. Healy was the county marshal and a man who knew how to get along as long as he was paid to do so.

"What did our marshal want?"

"His payoff, of course. After he got it, he mentioned that the State Police from the Western Barracks would be accompanying some Treasury Agents coming down to enforce the Volstead Act. He seemed to think this information deserved more money."

"Did you give it to him?"

"Nope, I thanked him, told him there'd be something coming when he gave us the word and said I'd see him next week. Now the federals can be bought, we've been paying off revenue men for years, but the State Police have their own code, and they follow it. They might not look too hard, but they will look. So it's best that we hide the product."

Burke thought for a moment. "How about taking it far into the woods? We leave it under guard, and after the feds and the state boys see that all we're selling is light cider and Coca-Cola, we bring it back."

"You don't want to put men in the woods, Paddy, not around here."

"Why not?"

He's not going to understand, Meadows thought. *City people, outsiders never do. Still, I have to try.*

And so Meadows told Burke about the snallygaster, the half-bird, half reptile who hunted from the sky and either ripped its prey apart or drained its blood. He told him about the dwayyo, who roamed in packs and ruled the ground. And he told Burke about what had happened to him and his boys some years past.

"That's why I'm here, Paddy. That's why we're all working for people like you and not cooking 'shine in the woods like we was raised to."

Burke heard him out. When Meadows was finished, he said, "Bullshit. We're in the twentieth century, Ray. The Modern Age. The Jazz Age. The only things that go bump in the night are guys and gals making whoopie. When Healy gives us the office, take the stuff out to the woods."

"We'll help you take it out if you do it in the daylight, Paddy. I'd advise against putting a guard on it...unless it's someone you don't care doesn't come back."

Burke shook his head. "Can't do it. Sala probably has people watching us. He may even have someone on the inside. I know I have people working for him. If he gets word we're moving product, he'll snatch it overnight. It will need guarding."

"Then have your men do it. Me and mine are staying here."

Burke saw that Meadows was not going to move on in this. "Okay, I'll send some of my boys and bring in some of the others."

Meadows nodded. "You know those hex signs you see around?"

"Yeah."

"When they go out, have your men take some with them. For some reason, snallygasters don't like them. This Dutch fellow I talked to once said the patterns do things to their mind."

Burke chuckled. *Knew he wouldn't believe me*, Meadows thought as the man said, "And what about these, what did you call them, dwayyos? These hexes work on them."

Meadows shook his head. "Nothing works on the dway except light. Best you can do is hope that there aren't that many of them and that you can run faster than the men you're with."

Again Burke chuckled. "Anything else, Ray?"

"Yeah, Paddy. Your man Moore tried to mess with one of the Walsh girls. You should tell him how the two of us first met."

It was just after the gangs moved in and Burke had opened his roadhouse. Some of his men had thought the local girls were theirs for the taking, so they did. Meadows volunteered to see Burke about it.

"What about it?" Burke had asked. Then he shrugged and said, "These things happen."

"That's your answer then?" a shocked Meadows asked.

"The only one you're gonna get."

"All right then," Meadows said calmly then left.

Burke smiled, thinking, This is going to be easy.

The three men who had assaulted the women were known. They hadn't tried to hide what they did, seeing they thought it their right as men. They were easily found and easily taken. The next day, Meadows again went to see Burke.

"Would you please step outside, Mr. Burke?"

Burke did, and saw the bodies of his three men. Two had taken gun blasts to their stomach, the other to his chest. "What the hell is this?"

"Sometimes, these things happen, Mr. Burke. The next time it might happen to you."

Burke nodded in understanding. Liking the way Meadows had handled things, he soon hired the man.

Remembering, Burke nodded and said, "I'll have a word with Moore. And when the time comes, I'll have him help guard the product."

"Sounds good to me. How fast can he run?"

"He's more than a mite slow."

Meadows smiled. "Sounds even better."

The next day, Duffy, Burke's manager, got the word from Marshal Healy. The state and federal men would be down at the end of the week.

"We need to move the stuff today," he said. They were at the bar, and today there was gin to be tasted. Duffy poured glasses for him and Meadows.

"What's the hurry, Duff?" Meadows asked.

Duffy took a sip, nodded in approval, and said, "Ray, you and I both know that Healy is the kind of marshal who knows what not to see as long as he gets paid not to see it. Hell, everyone in town knows. So it's likely the state boys know it too."

It made sense, and Meadows nodded in agreement. "So when they told Healy end of the week…"

"Ray, I'm surprised they're not already here. Get together who you can. We're moving the stuff today."

"Burke tell you what I told him?"

Duffy smiled. "About the monsters, yeah, he told me," he said with a laugh. *He doesn't believe me, either.* Meadows thought. *He will tomorrow, or the day after. Well, the damn fools were warned.*

"Duff, I know to you this sounds crazy, but at least put up the hex signs and build the fires high and bright."

"Why? So Sala's men will know where we are? You sure you're not working for him, Ray?" he asked jokingly as he reached under the bar. "I'd rather put my faith in this."

Duffy took out a weapon, one Meadows had heard about but had never seen. They called it a Thompson sub-machine gun.

CHAPTER THREE

Raphael Meadows spent the night on his front porch hoping, no praying, that he'd be wrong. He had helped move the crates of 'shine, gin, and cider that afternoon. The night was still, and the moon cast honest shadows on the ground. It reminded him how it was that last night he and the boys had spent in the woods and he could not repress a shiver. He told himself that the night was cool, but he knew that was a lie.

Meadows said a prayer for Burke's men though he didn't know them all that well. He worked with them but didn't know them. Given a choice, they weren't the kind of men he'd choose to know. But working for Burke, working with his men, was how he fed his family and so he did what any man would do, the best he could. Didn't mean he wished them ill, but better them than his kin.

With that, his thoughts came round to his family. His Mary, right now asleep in their warm featherbed. He should be with her, but worry kept him awake, drove him outside. She worried about him, worried about him working for Burke, about his job being on the gray side of legal. But nobody around where they lived worried too much about what the government said you could or couldn't do. There was nothing wrong with providing people what they'd been drinking all their lives. Or so Meadows told himself. And again, he knew he was lying.

Right now, it's peaceful, he thought. *But sooner or later, Sala's gonna want what Burke has, or Burke will want what Sala has. The guns their men carry aren't for hunting, they're for killing, especially that*

Thompson of Duffy's. You don't get something like that unless you expect to use it.

Again he thought of the night the dwayyo and the snally-gasters clashed. He had gotten himself and his boys out of those woods just in time. *Now I'm in another,* he realized. A different one, but one just as dangerous. Maybe it's time to leave this one.

Meadows decided he'd think about it, talk to Mary about what was right for them and the boys.

He didn't have to worry about his girls. Caitlan, although she preferred to be called Katie, was already married to Conor, a young man with a job in town as a butcher. Assistant butcher, that was, but he was saving up to buy into the business, the butcher not having any sons. Kevin, the boy Bridget was going with, seemed nice, and Meadows had already had "the talk" with him, the talk about respect and boundaries and how "no" meant "no" and how "maybe" meant "no" and how deep and final the woods could be for anyone who hurt his daughter in any way.

Thomas was doing well. He had a head for numbers that boy did. Burke had tried to get the boy to come work for him, keeping the books and maybe doing a bit of managing, but Meadows had steered his boy to the town bank and so had, in a way, gotten him away from the woods.

It was Sean that Meadows worried about. The boy liked guns a little too much and always seemed to hang around the roadhouse and the men who worked there. Meadows tried keeping his youngest with him, helping with distilling and bottling, but the boy always found his way to helping Duffy or one of the others.

Meadows had tried talking to Sean, telling him that there was right and there was wrong and that Burke's men either didn't know the difference or didn't care.

"Then why do you work for them, Da?"

Other than "just stay away from them," Meadows didn't have an answer to that. *Still don't,* he thought and decided to do what many men with such a problem did, take it to his wife.

This decision made, or at least put off, Meadows looked up toward the woods. The fires from the camps where the product was stored were like faint stars in the sky. "Not bright enough," he said aloud. Although he didn't like them much, they were men and did not deserve what might happen to them.

If it happened. Meadows reminded himself that a man could safely spend weeks in the woods without seeing the shadow of the dway or the snallygaster overhead. But just like the roulette wheel Burke was talking about putting in, sooner or later, his number was going to come up. And when it did, the only payoff would be death, with the red of blood mixing with the black of night. Best not to play at all.

Before Meadows could think about what bringing wheels and tables into the roadhouse might mean, there came a great howl from the woods. He barely heard it, but it was there. Another howl rose, followed by distant sounds of gunfire, and he knew that Burke's gamble had been lost.

There were strangers in the hunting grounds, invading the territory. Verr could smell them. They stank of prey, but there was something else. Thoughts of killing, but not hunting or eating. They were like and not like the others who had retreated, leaving the grounds to the pack.

Like the others, these men stood on their hind legs. Some carried the noisemakers that stung, hurt, and killed. But these had no fear, not of the pack, not of the dark, not of anything. They did not look for shadows. It was as if they did not know the pack or the dark. The others, the ones who knew the shadows, they kept the light bright, the light that hurt. These new ones had the light, but it did not hurt. It was small and weak—like them.

Verr listened and waited for the searchers to return. Soon they did, and by scent, sound, and mind told of the hated flying ones. They had smelled their odor and heard the beating of wings, not close but on the high ground near the nesting place. It was the flyers' time, the time to mate and make young. They would not wander far from their nest, and it was good not to get too close. Close meant becoming food for the flyers, and the pack was not food.

For a moment, Verr thought of the pack's mating time, when heat came from the females, and the urge came over the males. They would fight, but he would win, and the females would choose him. He'd take the ones who would give strong pups and leave the rest to the other strong, the ones who did not lead, to be chosen next. The weak ones would not be chosen, would not mate, and the pack would grow stronger.

Verr liked the mating time, but that time was not this time. Now was the time to hunt, kill, and grow strong on the meat of the prey.

He sent the young ones to sniff out their prey. They came back. The prey had divided into several groups, with not many men in each.

As untrained pups, they were. Better to have one pack of many than divide your strength. Even the forest prey knows that. Together is strength; together means only the weakest are lost to the pack. Separate means more are lost, more food for the pack.

Verr sent out his thoughts, telling which hunters to take which group. He would take the young, unblooded ones.

He waited, waited until mind and scent told him they were ready.

Now is the time, he sent, and the pack projected fear into the minds of the prey. Then, again as one, the pack let out its howl and charged into the midst of the strangers.

Men and pack met. Some noisemakers went off, and Verr felt two hunters leave the pack. But then the pack swarmed its prey — clawing it, biting it, bringing the prey down, ripping it open, and lapping its blood.

Some of the men ran. The young thought to pursue, but Verr snarled them back. *Let them go. Do not leave the pack,* he growled at them. *Safety is only with the pack.* They were young, they would learn, or they would leave the pack.

Verr was the first to eat. He took a bite from each of the bodies then chose the most savory as his own, leaving the others to fight over what he had left.

As he ripped the covering off his meat, as he tore into the soft flesh of its middle, Verr heard growls of challenge come from the other two parts of the pack. Once dominance was established, the members of the pack, each in its turn, feasted. Once they could devour no more, they returned to the packhome, leaving the remainder to the lesser creatures that scavenged their leavings.

When they heard the growls, when the shadows came toward them, when they saw the two-legged horrors coming toward them, Burke's men knew that the stories the locals had been telling were true. They also knew that there was nothing much they could do about it now. Some knowledge came too late. A few of them stood their ground and fired their guns, but only Duffy's Tommy might have stopped them, and Duffy had not seen fit to lend it to them.

Men died, their throats ripped open and their guts torn out. Others turned and ran. Some were caught, bought down, and dragged back before feeling sharp teeth and sharper claws tear into them.

Three escaped, leaving the screams and cries of their comrades behind them as they ran blindly into the woods. Stumbling through the brush, tripping over branches, the three left a trail a nearly blind dog with very little nose could have followed. But the pack no longer had an interest in them. Still, the three men ran and kept running until they could run no more. They stopped to rest, but on hearing what they thought were dim sounds of pursuit but were only the faint noises of the pack devouring their friends, they ran some more.

Finally, they had to stop.

"Where the hell are we?" Moore asked, looking around once he had caught his breath.

"Who cares? We're alive, that's all that matters," Dunne answered.

"For how long? I think it's best we go back."

Dunne almost yelled, "Go back? Are you crazy, Walsh?" but not wanting to attract, well, anything, said it just above a whisper. "Those *things* are still back there." He gestured to the pinpoints of light that showed where their camps had been. "And some of them may be coming for us."

"If those things were still after us, we'd be dead by now," Moore argued. "So let's see if we get our bearings and find us a way around them."

"I think it's best if we find a place to hide for the night and go back during the day."

Dunne and Moore thought Walsh's idea a good one. "That hill over there. Let's try that. The higher ground and all that. We should be safe there." Dunne said, none of them seeing the shadow that passed high overhead.

Forra had flown his flight and had been embraced by Kona, whose tentacles had enveloped him to suck not his blood but his essence. She took it inside herself, and from it, she made her eggs. Four of them, two like Forra, two like her. She now sat on them, covering them, warming them, protecting them. When they hatched, she would feed and teach them. The ones that learned, the ones that survived, would leave the nest when ready. Then she and Forra would rest and sleep. Once they awoke, they would again dance in the moonlight, and the cycle would repeat.

Kona's job was to protect the eggs and the nest. Forra's was to protect and feed her. Each night he flew and hunted for prey, his great wings spread against the sky. Some nights the woods yielded food, sometimes small prey, sometimes larger. Once, his iron-like claws had snatched one of the hairy ones that had become separated from its pack. It clawed and scratched and bit but, holding it fast, Forra rose high and let it fall. Then he flew down to where it lay, ripped it open, and took the sweet insides back to her, eating only when she had fully fed.

Only when the woods did not give up prey did he travel to the flat land where there was plenty of prey but also danger.

Creatures much like the hairy ones. These men had images that hurt his eyes and confused his mind. Once, during a previous flight, Forra saw humans on the flat land not protected by the dreaded image. He swooped down and grabbed a young one. The older ones sent fire and pain his way. Still, he managed to bring it back to Kona. She embraced it and drained it, after which he ate its flesh. It was not very good. So mostly, he avoided humans, flying high over them, only swooping down on the herds of the placid cattle to grab the choicest of them.

That night Forra heard the dwayyo. Some came close but soon departed. Later he heard the pack in the low woods. Not wanting to fly too far away from Kona, he let them be, let them feed. But shortly after their growling ceased, there came the ones like them, the humans. From above, he circled them. They took no notice and began to ascend his hill. Remembering the fire and the pain, he quickly descended.

The first died quickly, disemboweled by his hooked claw. The other two ran, or tried to. He quickly caught them, one in each claw. Flying up to the nest, he dropped them close to his mate.

Kona fed well that night, wrapping a tentacle around each of them, draining them dry, leaving him the meat. It still was not very good, but he ate it anyway. Later that week, he would hunt fat cattle.

The bodies were found late the following morning, after the state and the treasury men had come, looked around, and left without finding anything but some corn mash. There was nothing illegal about that, but they took it anyway.

Meadows knew he should have had Burke send someone first thing, but it would not have done the dead men any good and might have caused trouble with the government men, trouble he'd be involved in.

"Sala's men?" Duffy asked hopefully as he, Burke, Meadows, and some others looked over the camps at what was left of the bodies.

"Men don't do this," Burke said. "All the drink is here, and look at the tracks; it was wolves or something."

"Look at the tracks again, Paddy," Meadows answered. "The beasts that left them walks on two legs. Look at the wounds— sharp claws and teeth." He reached down and pulled something up, something black that was stuck in dried blood. "This is from one of them. More hair than fur. And the attacks, all three camps, probably all at once. Wolves don't... *can't* plan like that."

"What are you saying, Ray?" Duffy asked.

Answering Duffy but looking at Burke, Meadows said, "You know what I'm saying."

Burke nodded. "You're saying this was the dwayyo." Meadows nodded. "You're saying that I should have listened to you." Another nod. "You're saying that I sent these men to their deaths."

This time there was no nod. But neither did Meadows offer any words of consolation or absolution. This guilt was on Burke's conscience, assuming he had one.

"What should we do?" Burke asked.

To Meadows, the answer was obvious. "You wrap them up, take them down, and give their bodies to their families, if they have any in these parts. You treat them decent, you pay for proper funerals and burials, and you give their families whatever these men are due and maybe more, given that they died for you." He looked at the cases of drink. "For this."

"No, I meant, what should we do about the dwayyo?"

It's as if he hasn't heard a word I said. He still doesn't understand and probably never will. It's time to get out. Mary's got family in Baltimore. We can go there. To Burke, Meadows said, "It's like this, Paddy. The way I understand it, you've got your territory down here, and Sala's got his north of the city. You don't go into his, and he doesn't go into yours. If you do, people will probably get hurt or dead. This here," Meadows waved his hand around the camp, "is dwayyo territory, and up there," he pointed towards the hills, "belongs to the snallygaster. We stay out of their territory, and if we don't," he looked at the bodies, "more men will die like this."

Before Burke could reply, a man came from one of the other sites and said something to Duffy, who came over. "We're missing three bodies, Paddy. We count nine. There should be twelve. Looks like they ran off in that direction." Duffy pointed to the hills. Both he and Burke looked toward Meadows.

"If they don't come back, chances are the snallys have got them. Now you can go look if you want, but if that's so," again Meadows looked at the bodies, "these men died easy compared to what the snallygasters would do to them. As for me and mine, we'll take care of the bodies. You can bring down what they died for."

A week after the funerals and burials, with empty coffins representing the three lost men, Raphael Meadows called his family together.

"Burke's told me his plans," he said to them. "He's bought into two more roadhouses, the ones outside Lambert and Baxter. He's going to expand them, hoping to bring in people from Harbor City. But he says that will take more than just 'shine and the soft stuff to bring those people in. So he's going to start serving meals and having music along with wheels, dice, and card tables. He says the games will be on the level. Maybe they will, maybe not. We'll see. He's also be getting beer and bottles of whiskey and the like."

Meadows shook his head. "There's gonna be trouble. More attention from the Prohibition agents. That doesn't bother me. Their kind have their price. It's the other gangs."

Meadows paused, took a breath, thought about how to say what needed saying.

"It'll be peaceful for a while, but all these people want is more. If the money comes in like Burke thinks it will, they'll be more blood and death than the creatures in the woods ever caused. We can keep out of the way of those things. There's no keeping away from greedy men with guns."

Meadows studied his family. Once he felt that what he had said had sunk in, "I've decided to get out while we still can.

Mary's cousin James says he can get me a manager's job at an A&P in Baltimore. After helping to run the roadhouse, I think I can handle it. Thomas, James said they also need accountants and that banks aren't as safe as people think they are. Conor, I know you and Katie have a life here, but a good butcher can always find work. I'm sure the A&P can use you," he said with a smile.

Meadows interrupted his younger daughter before she could raise her obvious objection, "Bridget, don't say a word. I know you and Kevin are close. Don't tell me how close or I may have to take the boy for a walk in the woods and come back alone. You are coming with us. If your young man loves you enough, he can come with us. He's welcome as long as you and he behave. We can find him something."

"He says he wants to join the police force," Bridget said sullenly.

"Well," Meadows replied. 'Well, maybe, if he can't find an honest job."

"What about me, Da?" asked Sean, who seemed even less pleased than his sister. "Can I stay here?"

Meadows "NO!" came out a bit stronger than he had intended. "You're coming with us. Between James and me, I'm sure we can find you something."

Burke took the news well. "We'll miss you, Ray, but I can see why you're leaving. As much as I hate to admit it, you're too honest and good a man for what's coming. But just remember, if anyone comes asking around…"

"Not a word they'll get from me except 'Yes, I worked for you' and 'No, I didn't see anything.' If they ask what I did, I'll tell them I was your snallygaster hunter and they'll think I'm crazy."

The two men shook. "Thanks, Ray. Take care."

"You too, Paddy."

As he left the roadhouse for the last time, Meadows thought of Duffy's Tommy gun and wondered how bad things would get.

CHAPTER FOUR

A week went by, then two. One day four men came into Marshal Healy's office. One wore a cheap suit and had the look of a man trying to do a good job for a lost cause in which he didn't believe. *Has to be a treasury man*, Healy thought. The other two wore the uniform of the State Police — olive pants with a back stripe, tan shirt with a black tie, a Stetson hat, and a Sam Browne belt on which they holstered their service revolvers. These troopers had the look of men who had dedicated their lives to a cause and were willing to kill for it or die for it, in that order. These men scared Healy for he never had been, nor would he ever be that kind of man.

The fourth man wore civilian dress, but he wore it as if it were a uniform. *Some kind of cop*, Healy decided.

"Good afternoon, gentlemen," Healy said. "How can I help you?"

"We need to talk in your office, Healy," said one of the troopers who wore sergeant stripes and whose name tag read "Tabor." Healy noticed that the sergeant had not used his title but decided not to make an issue of it.

He led them into his office. Knowing enough not to offer them a drink from the bottle in his bottom desk drawer, he invited them to sit. They declined. Instead, with the Prohibition agent hanging near the door, the other three encircled him, the trooper and sergeant in front of his desk, the unknown man to the side, effectively trapping Healy in his own office.

"Just what the hell is this all about?" Healy asked, his voice mostly bluff with a trace of fear.

"*Marshal* Healy," the sergeant began, biting out the "Marshal" as if it left a bad taste in his mouth. "Other than the troopers involved and Agent Stack here, the only person who knew about our inspection plans was you. Earlier surveillance had indicated that cider, gin, and moonshine were readily available in all of the roadhouses. Yet all we found at any of them was soft cider and Coca-Cola."

Surprisingly, Sergeant Tabor did not ask the usual follow-up questions, such as "Why do you think that was so?" or "How do you explain that?" He just stood there in silence until Healy caught on.

"If you knew that booze was being served, why didn't you act...oh, I see. You weren't interested in the booze or who was selling it, were you? It was me, wasn't it?"

Sergeant Tabor nodded his head so slightly that his Stetson barely moved. "These are difficult times. Lawmen are being required to enforce a law that was imposed by a minority, and with which most of the people in the country disagree. The governor understands and expects a certain...laxity in enforcement. But he does not expect his marshals to sell their badges."

Removing a piece of paper from inside his uniform shirt, Sergeant Tabor handed it to Healy. "Charles Healy, by order of the governor, an order countersigned by the county executive, you are hereby relieved of your duties as marshal of Corbett County."

There was nothing for Healy to do. He had gotten too greedy and now was paying the price. He thought about what he might do next. Maybe Burke or Sala would find a place for him. But no, he had betrayed one master for money, so they could not be sure that he would not betray them. Gathering his personal belongings, he said, "I'll send for my clothes when I get settled, somewhere." With no vehicle, no home, and little money saved up from salary and bribes, he left a broken man.

When the trooper who had accompanied Sergeant Tabor offered Healy a ride, Healy said, "Take me to the Dunkirk Hotel."

It wasn't the best in town, but it was a place to think about what to do next. As the trooper's car approached it, Healy asked, "Who was that other guy?"

"Your replacement."

Unlike the short, portly Healy, Russell Thorne was tall and solidly built, and the way he carried his gun told everyone that he knew how to use it.

Thorne had been a police officer in Coast City, where rum-running and bootlegging had replaced tourism as the city's main industry. Knowing he could do nothing to stem the tide of illegal alcohol coming in by sea and going out by car, truck, and rail, Thorne concentrated on the violence that accompanied the criminal enterprise and punishing those who caused it.

He was a smart cop, one who knew that in the times in which he lived, arrests did not always lead to convictions, and convictions did not always send criminals to jail, especially ones who were connected to men of wealth and influence. So he made sure that when he did make arrests, they would stick. As for those men who were considered above the law, sometimes they were released despite the evidence. Other times, they were buried, when Thorne had enough evidence to justify his shooting them in self-defense.

His actions got him noticed. He was hailed as a crusader by some newspapers and called a killer by others. He was definitely considered an irritant by those men, elected and otherwise, who ran the city. Since he could not be bought and would not be silenced, and since killing him or any other police officer was just not done, the powers that be appealed to the governor and Russell Thorne was promoted.

Two days after his appointment as Marshal of Corbett County, Thorne stopped in the Bixby House to introduce himself.

"Let's make things clear, Mr. Burke. Right now, I don't care about the Volstead Act, or who drinks what, or where they drink it. And if you're going to have gambling, keep the games honest, and pay off when you lose. And no doxies. If I hear of any dame showing it or selling it, I'll close you down. If I hear that you're peddling dope, I'll burn this place down with your dead body inside it. Understand?"

Burke had heard much the same speech from Healy when those two had first met, only Healy had not expressed himself as forcefully.

"Understood. And speaking of understanding, Marshal, Healy and me, we had one."

The look Thorne gave Burke was one of total disgust, as if the man were dog crap he had just scraped from his boot.

"Mr. Burke, I'm paid by the county to be the law around here. Our only arrangement is that you follow the county and state laws as I've explained them to, or I'll make you sorry you didn't. And I work with the State Police, not against them."

"Again, Marshal, understood." When Thorne stood to leave, Burke said, "Drink before you go, Marshal?"

There was no smile on Thorne's face as he answered, "Haven't you heard, Mr. Burke, that's against the law."

Thorne got in his car and started driving back to his office in Dunkirk, the county seat. *That went about as well as it did with Sala,* he thought. *It's peaceful now but not for much longer. Burke has his three in Bixby, Lambert, and Baxter. Sala has his two in Holden and Blair. There are a few independents that'll be gone once the gambling and hard stuff comes in. They'll shut down or sell out, although the one here outside of Dunkirk might last a while longer. I don't think either Burke or Sala wants to be that close to the Marshal's office. Then the fighting will start — the raids, the gunfire, the deaths. All over something that they shouldn't be selling and people shouldn't be drinking. Soon there will be one man running things, and they'll each want to be that man. Hope that gets settled without too many bodies, but I doubt it. Once it's done, I'll take care of whoever is left. After that, there will be The Almighty's Peace in this county.*

Then he added, *Of course, even The Almighty sometimes needs a little help.*

One of the benefits of Thorne's job was that his office had an apartment on the third floor for his use, so he didn't have to pay for a place to sleep. "Of course, you'll always be at work," said the deputy who had welcomed him and showed him around.

Thorne wasn't married, nor did he have anyone special in his life. "Doesn't matter," he said, "I'm always at work."

Thorne had just left. Burke was sitting at a back table when Duffy came out from the back. "You heard?"

"Yeah, Paddy, I heard. Think that was just air?"

"What I think, Duff, is that this Thorne means business, *his* business and not ours. But this is not a small county, and he's just one man with a few deputies who like a little extra every two weeks. We'll be okay as long as we make sure to clean up our own mess before he hears about it."

"What about the girls?"

"We can run them out of houses in the towns. Keep the businesses separate. We'll just have to makes sure that the town cops get their piece…of everything."

Whatever Duffy was going to say, that was interrupted by a knock on the door. Duffy and Burke looked at each other, then Duffy called out, "We don't open until six."

More knocking, this time more insistent. "Get the bar, Duff."

Duffy went behind the bar, picked up the shotgun that was kept there, and made sure it was loaded. He nodded at Burke, who went over to the front door and unlocked it. Stepping to one side, he opened the door.

In walked Sean Meadows.

Pulling the young man inside, Burke first looked outside to see if anyone had come with him. Seeing no one else, he shut and locked the door.

"Your father know you're here, Sean?"

Sean shrugged. "By now, he's read the note I left. But that said I'd be catching a freight train west. Course he still might call the marshal's office to see if I'm here."

"Why are you here?" Burke asked, thinking he already knew the answer.

"Mr. Burke, I hate Baltimore. We live in a little house attached to other houses. I have to sleep in the basement with my sister's boyfriend and pretend to be asleep when she sneaks down so they can, well, you know. And all I do all day is stock shelves and clean up in the A&P store. I couldn't take it no more, so I wrote my note, got together what money I could, and hitched my way here."

"Again, Sean, why here? What do you want from me?"

"I figured that after what happened in the woods, you were still short of men. Take me on, Mr. Burke, and I'll do anything you say. Anything at all."

There was a look in the young man's eyes that Burke had seen before. It was a look of passion and hunger and need. It was a predator's look that caused Burke to think of the dwayyo he'd been told about. *If there's a human equivalent, it's this boy*, he thought. And he knew that if he brought Sean into his gang, his pack, the boy would do whatever he was asked. He'd kill for his pack or die for his pack, and it wouldn't matter to him which it was.

"Sean, your father is a smart man. He'll figure you came here and either write or try to phone the marshal. But the marshal's new and has never seen you. So from now on, you're John, no, Jack Reilly. You're my cousin, and you work for me. Duffy, get a drink for our new friend."

Thorne's apartment had a balcony off the kitchen. He liked to sit out on it for twenty minutes or so before turning in. That night, after visiting Burke, as he looked out over the woods and mountains in the distance, he heard the sound of a train whistle then watched as something large with wings transited the Moon.

Chapter Five

Vincent Sala was a smart man. He was smart enough to get in with the Tomas gang in Harbor City. And smart enough to get out when it started dealing in flesh rather than booze.

He made a deal with the Martinellis. They were more his kind of people anyway. He told them about his idea for roadhouses outside the smaller towns.

"The Irish are already starting with them. Can't let them have all the fun, or the money."

In exchange for a cut, Sala got the okay, funding, and a promise of help if he needed it.

He now had two houses outside of Blair and Holden. Like Burke in the south, he started slow and was now expanding them. But two was not enough for Vincent Sala. His vision was a ring of places around Harbor City, offering the city dwellers a sense of adventure to go along with the thrill of breaking an unjust and unpopular law. True, they could get that at any speak in the city, but going to a roadhouse, well, that was a night out. In addition, roadhouses provided couples who were married but not to each other more or less discrete places to go, and there were plenty of dark spots on the way home.

Of course, Sala's roadhouse empire did not yet include Patrick Burke's three houses or the independents who would not be able to compete with either of them. But right then, Sala was content to maintain the peace and leave things as they were. Let Burke do the work and spend the money on the Bixby, the Lambert, and the

Baxter. Once they were up and running and showing a profit, then Sala would take them away from him.

The newly-christened Jack Reilly was on night duty, patrolling the area around the Bixby Roadhouse. He liked the dark now that his nightmares about the shadows in the woods had stopped. What was it his father had called them? The dway. Others called them dwayyo. They were said to be scary monsters.

Jack held the shotgun Burke had given him. It was a pump-action, 12-gauge Winchester Model 12. *Better than the old double-barrel Da and us used. If we had had this that night…*

He imagined holding the Winchester, pumping and firing as the dwayyo attacked. They would be the ones running, not him and his family. He tightened his grip on the weapon. The thought of one day using it excited him and made him feel strong. He wondered if he would ever get the chance. Maybe if there were a prowler or a raid. He hoped so.

A whisper in the dark. "Sean Meadows."

On hearing his old name, Jack turned first right then left. A quiet laugh.

"Relax, Sean. If I had wanted you dead, you'd be grave fill by now."

"Who are you? What do you want?" Jack asked, wondering what he should do. Call out or keep the intruder talking. If he were an intruder. He decided to wait. Maybe the man would do something to give away his position. Then he could use the Winchester.

"I'm a friend of Paddy Burke's, Jack. That's how I know your real name. He sent me out here to talk to you in quiet, away from the other men. He knows he can trust you, that he can count on you. He's gonna need things done he doesn't want others to know about and figures you're the man for the job."

"Things like what?"

"Things that will give you a chance to use the gun your holding."

It took all Jack had to keep the excitement from his voice. "Sounds good."

"It may involve killing."

"Sounds better. Just tell me where, when, and how many."

"Knew we could count on you, Jack." A white envelope hit the ground in front of Jack. "A little extra from Paddy. Don't tell the others, and don't mention it to him."

Jack waited but soon realized he was again alone. He picked up the envelope, stuffed it in his pocket. He'd count it later. Maybe there'd be enough for a trip into Bixby. He gripped his gun tighter and resumed his patrol, unaware that he was still being watched.

On the edge of the woods, hidden by the trees, with not even the light of the Moon to cast their shadow and reveal their presence, Verr and two of the young ones watched. Something had called the pack leader, something that spoke of coming danger, like the change in the air before the lightning flashed and the thunder roared. It felt like another predator, one both like and unlike the pack.

Above, he heard the cry of a flying one. It was out hunting, as he would have been but for the call. What he had felt was neither of the flying ones.

Verr looked into the open area. He saw a man who held the thing that made thunder and caused death. He sensed another man, one who hid in the shadows. These were not hunters; they were the hunted. He thought of sending the young ones down for their first kill. But he did not want to lose them to the thunder.

Let them be blooded another way. As he led them away, he again heard the whistle of the flying one. Hs scouts had told him that the female had just hatched her eggs.

Good, he thought. *We will wait for them to grow, and then they will make a nice feast for the pack.*

From above came a screech of anger, and the snallygaster swooped the lowest Verr had ever seen. Almost brushing the treetops, it screeched again as it circled where they stood.

Or maybe not, Verr thought. *There is easier game,* he decided, like men who gathered in the dark. One day I will lead the pack into the open, and we will feed on them.

There were no cattle out that night—the humans were learning—and Forra was about to fly to the other side of the high ground to hunt for forest game when he felt the disturbance, the unease of the dwayyo. Flying high, he called out to Kona, then turned and followed the feeling.

The dwayyo were at the edge of the woods. Like them, Forra saw one human and sensed the other one. The thoughts of the young one, the one in the open, were mixed, at first wary, then as excited as a male before his first dance. The thoughts of the other were dark and full of menace.

Had the younger one not been carrying the thunder maker, Forra would have swooped and taken him. Another night, an approach from behind, a slash to remove the limb, he promised himself, even if humans did not taste that good.

Forra was about to return to his hunt when the largest of the dwayyo thought of attacking the nest. Enraged, he flew as low as he could. Had the dwayyo not been protected by the trees, he would have grabbed one of them and torn it to pieces right there. It would have been a waste of meat and blood, but still, it would have been satisfying.

Flying off, Forra made himself another promise, that one night he would find the hairy ones' den, carry off *their* young, and he and Kona would feast on them.

Sala was again looking over the reports he had received from his man inside Burke's organization about the strange creatures seen outside Bixby.

"You would be wise to leave things alone, Mr. Burke," Sala said out loud. He had learned about the snallygasters and the dwayyo from some of his men. His native land was not troubled by such things, if one excepted the Tatzelwurm in the north, but it had been over a hundred years since one of them had been seen, and so was about as much of a myth as the minotaur, the centaur, and the Pegasus. *What was it about America that breeds such monsters?* Sala thought. The Martinellis had tried to bring liquor from Mexico through the Chesapeake Bay only to have their ships destroyed by what the only survivor described as a leviathan. It made him think of the monster of Lake Como, but that too was the stuff of tales and children's stories. The only monsters that had ever haunted Lake Como were named Frankenstein, and that family was long dead. Or so it was hoped.

As Sala was thinking these thoughts, his aide, Anthony Ricci came in.

"Ah, Anthony, I was just about to call you. What are our plans to bring in the real stuff? The whiskey they make in Harbor City tastes like colored tea into which someone has poured grain alcohol. And not enough alcohol at that. The beer is okay, but the rest..." He shook his head.

Anthony Ricci was a nice young man. Born in America to immigrant parents, he had the classic Sicilian features that attracted all the girls. That Anthony was not attracted to the girls was of no concern to Ricci, as long as the boy did his job and was discrete.

"As you know, Mr. Sala, shipments in the bay have been suspended, but there are plans to unload outside Virginia Beach and truck the stuff north. Only the routes have to be worked out and arrangements to be made with the families down there as well as the police."

Sala nodded his understanding, then indicated for Ricci to continue.

"Thanks to the Coast Guard working with the Treasury, shipments from Coast City have stopped. It might take a few weeks before they resume. It's just a matter of figuring who to pay off and how much. Still, there's the Canadian stuff Martinelli's sending us. It's coming through New York State. It will be nice to have the real McCoy to sell to our customers."

"Maybe not the whole McCoy, Anthony. We'll mix it half and half with the local stuff. By this time, no one remembers what the good stuff tastes like, so we should be okay. What about Burke?"

"Once it opens up again, the Coast City organization will sell to anyone with cash. And they'll cut off anyone who tries to hijack any of their customers. Like us, Burke has arrangements with brewers and distillers in Harbor City. And from what our man says, it looks as if he might be unloading some Mexican stuff somewhere near Westover on the James River. No Canadian connection yet, but our source tells us that he'll be trying a Rhode Island landing later this week, running the stuff through Connecticut and Pennsylvania."

"Thank you, Anthony. Let us concentrate on securing our own supply lines. Inform our New England friends, let them intercept Burke's trucks. Otherwise, we shall leave Mr. Burke alone for now. After all, his current success is our future gain."

The trucks were halfway through Connecticut when two state police cruisers pulled them over. It was only after the drivers got out of their cabs that they realized that while the cars were the real thing, the men who had gotten out of them were not. On seeing the rifles and shotguns, the four men slowly raised their hands.

"You carrying?" asked the hijacker who seemed to be in charge.

As one, all of Burke's men shook their heads. "No load is worth dying for," one said.

"It's not worth killing for either," said the chief hijacker. He pointed down the road. "Walk that way, Sooner or later, you'll be able to flag someone down. If not, New Haven's less than a day's walk. Better still," he took the keys to the two trooper cars and threw them into the woods. "Find them and you can ride back in style. Maybe when you return them, you'll get a reward."

"Or locked up for stealing them."

The hijacker nodded. "There is that. I guess you four better start walking then."

As Burke's men walked off in one direction, the hijackers drove off in the other.

"They'll be coming down from Canada," Patrick Burke said, "two men per truck. There are too many back roads for the feds and the state police to watch all of them, even if they wanted to. From what I hear, they'll be five trucks. The first will be a decoy, filled with legitimate merchandise. The others will have legit stuff, with the booze behind a false wall in the back. If the decoy gets through, it's safe for the others. If it gets stopped, the rest will scatter, and maybe some make it. It's a new route, so it should be safe. Speaking of which, how did the Rhode Island run go, Duff?"

Duffy shook his head. "Stopped midway through Connecticut, as we expected."

"Then that problem's solved. Let's be more careful who we hire in the future."

Burke then addressed the men he had assembled. In those dark days of Prohibition, there was plenty of work for men with guns and the willingness to use them. Those before him were such men, some hand-picked from his roadhouse crews, others supplied by his backers, all men who could be trusted to do the job they were given without question or scruples.

Burke pointed to a map on the table.

"You'll pick up the trucks here." He indicated a spot in Pennsylvania.

"Mr. Burke?"

"Yes, Jack, what is it?"

Jack Reilly, formerly Sean Meadows, was on the crew going out. This would be his first job, a job where he would either prove himself or show yellow. If the first, then well and good. If the second, best to know now. There were other jobs an eager young man could do.

"Why are we stopping the trucks in Pennsylvania? Why not let them come down? Plenty of places around here to unload safely, and the barn is ready."

Burke smiled. "Jackie, my boy, whoever said these are our trucks?" He then dismissed the men. "Get what sleep you can, boys. An early start tomorrow so you can be set up by the evening." As they left, he called out, "Dylan, stay a minute." Then, on a sudden impulse, "you too, Jackie."

It was the four of them—Jack and Dylan sitting with Burke at his table, Duffy cleaning up after the others. Duffy almost wished that Jack would fail his test. He could use some more help in the roadhouse. *I'm the manager*, he thought. *I should not be doing this.* But he knew why that night he was.

"What is it, Mr. Burke?"

Burke liked Jack, liked his eagerness, liked the respectful, almost worshipful way he called him "Mr. Burke." It was a shame about this job. Jobs like this could easily go bad. If this one did, it could change the young man, and not for the better. That's why he called him back. Best to get these things over with.

"Just listen, for now, Jackie. Dylan, we lost the shipment from our Rhode Island test run. It was only soda water we use for mixer, but still, it was money out of pocket. Yet it was money well spent. Because only three people knew about it—Duffy, me, and you. Why do you think that is?"

Dylan, who as a redhead was naturally very light-skinned, managed to turn even paler than he was. "I, I don't know, Paddy."

"Might it have anything to do with the fact that your mother's maiden name is Bianchi, or that she's related to the Riccis, who are well-connected to Vincent Sala?"

"Paddy. Mr. Burke, I assure you..."

"Don't bother, Dylan. I'm sure you're smart enough to know that I would not be asking questions I don't know the answers to. But I understand divided loyalties and all that. So tell me the truth, and I promise that I will not do anything to you." Dylan nodded in agreement. "Good, now how long have you been working for Sala."

"J-just a few months. I met Anthony Ricci and he told me how I could make some money and help our family."

"Family first, I like that, Dylan. Thank you for your honesty."

Burke nodded, and Dylan felt the cold barrel of a revolver against the back of his neck.

"Now I did tell you that I would not do anything to you, but I'm not the only man you betrayed, so I'll leave your fate in the hands of others. Duffy, Jackie, what should be done with Dylan?"

From behind him, Dylan heard, "We take him with us. Leave him with the rest. A friendly warning to Sala that we're on to him. Friendly this time, at least."

"Sounds good, Duff. Jackie, what do you think?"

Here was the test. Burke knew it, Jack knew it. How he responded would show what he was capable of.

"Mr. Burke, Mr. Duffy's plan is a good one, but leaving Dylan with the others will tell Sala that we were responsible for taking his trucks."

"That's true. So what do you suggest?"

Jack Reilly's face lit up, almost shining in eager anticipation. "The dwayyo are running again. Sometimes at night, when I'm on guard, I stand near the edge of the woods and listen for them. I've heard them the last three nights. Let's give this traitor to them."

His smile as he said this scared even Burke.

CHAPTER SIX

Dylan felt a blow to the head, and that was the last he knew before waking up in the woods. He was bound to a tree near the remains of an old still. He had deep cuts on his arms and legs, the blood flowing freely. If the dwayyo did not come, he'd still be dead by morning.

Shadows gathered, drawn by the scent of blood. Any hope Dylan had of a slow but easy death was dashed when he heard the growls. The pack came, and Dylan screamed, but not for long.

Verr could not understand why the men would give up one of their own. The pack did not do that, did not leave behind those that were hurt or the bodies of those who had left the pack. Maybe it was bait. Men had done that before.

Trapped beasts, tied, and kept from moving too far. Their fear calling the pack and others to it.

Once, before the pack had come to the woods, before Verr was the leader, a littermate had ventured too close to something that bleated in fright.

Easy prey, he had told Verr. Easy food that we do not have to share.

Not to share with the pack was not the way. They had found it, they would get a portion, but the whole pack must feed.

Verr hung back. His brother, who was sometimes braver but ofttimes more foolish than he, went forward. He was almost to the bleater when thunder boomed out. His brother fell, and two twos of men came from hiding.

Verr watched them from where he was hidden. He felt his brother as he left the pack. From the men he felt fear, confusion, amazement, and wonder. One thought of packs and of a hunt.

As much as Verr wanted to attack the men and rip their bodies apart, he knew that his duty was to warn the pack. They would have felt his brother leave them but would not know where or why. He rushed off, making no noise that the men could hear, sending his thoughts ahead.

He found the pack, or rather they found him by scent, sound, and mind. He told the one who was leader what had occurred and was cuffed to the ground for leaving the pack.

The next time you will not be welcomed back, *he was told.* Now show us.

The men were as foolish as his brother had been. They still stood near his body. As one, the pack felt their intention to conceal the body and hope the bleater attracted another.

Instead, the whole pack descended on them. None were given a chance to use their thunder.

The dead men and the bleater were dragged back to the packhome. The pack ate well that night, all but Verr. For hunting by day and for endangering the pack, he was made to wait until all were finished. Only then was he permitted the scraps.

Verr remembered this time as he looked upon the helpless man. The smell of his blood and his flesh called to him as well as the others in the pack. He restrained them. He sent out scouts and searched with his mind. No danger. Perhaps, like in the old times, it was an offering. If so, it was accepted. This time, Verr ate first.

Burke stood alone in the night, at the edge of the woods where Jack Reilly said he had heard the dwayyo. He stood there long after the growls and the screams had stopped. *I was wrong,* he thought as he watched Jack return. *This job is not going to change Jackie Reilly. He's already broken.*

Even knowing he would not sleep, Jack readied himself for bed. He was just about to get undressed when he heard pebbles against his window. Thinking back to that night when he was on guard duty, he left his second-floor room, went outside, and waited.

"Sean."

The whisper from the shadows sounded like the same one. For no reason at all, Jack thought it might be Burke himself, or maybe Duffy.

"The name's Jack," he said.

"I call you Sean so you'll know who I am."

"I don't know who you are."

"You know enough. Paddy wants you to do a special job, one none of the other men you're going with are willing or able to do." When the man in the shadows told Jack what it was, a thrill ran through the young man. "When it's done, here's what you say and do."

Another envelope hit the ground. "Paddy's thanks to you, Sean. And remember, not a word to anyone, not to Paddy, not even to yourself."

By the time Jack had picked up his payment, the man in the shadows was gone.

The Pennsylvania hijacking went as Burke had planned. As whiskey-laden trucks drove south on the York Road, his men let the decoy go past, then cut off the rest. A truck driven by one of Burke's men quickly got behind the decoy so as not to arouse the suspicion of its driver. Burke's driver would turn off in a few miles. By then, it would be too late.

The convoy drivers knew this might happen. The hijacking of trucks and the theft of their cargo had been around since shortly after goods began to be transported by land. The truckers knew what to do—keep your hands in plain sight, make no sudden moves, and follow instructions. Whatever was in the back of the truck was not worth a life, especially yours. So when their trucks were stopped and men with guns ordered the drivers out, they slowly left their cabs, making sure to keep their hands in plain sight.

It was only when the eight men were lined up along the side of the road that things went wrong. There was a shout of "He's got a gun!" and then the firing started.

Jack Reilly was the first to fire, his well-placed blasts from his pump-action shotgun quickly accounting for three of the men. Before these could hit the ground, before their fellow truckers could flee, Burke's other men pulled their revolvers and let them speak. Soon there were eight dead men on the road.

"What the hell happened?" yelled Pete Gallagher, the leader of the land pirates.

"One of them pulled a gun," Jack said, pointing to a revolver on the ground near the first men he shot.

"Anyone else see anything?" Gallagher asked. No one had.

"Damn it, well, get them into the woods and let's get the hell out of here before anyone comes by."

Bodies hidden, the four trucks followed the York Road for a time.

Jack was riding with Gallagher. "Watch the boy," Burke had said, and so the crew chief kept Jack close to him. After seeing how the kid had smiled at the sight of the bodies and not quite sure the kid hadn't just shot them for the fun of it, Gallagher decided that after this night's work, he'd watch him from a distance.

"Nasty work," Gallagher said, just before he turned his truck on to a dusty side road to make his way back to Bixby. "But I guess it couldn't be helped."

"No, it couldn't," Jack agreed, "but it wasn't so bad." Glancing over, Gallagher saw that the kid still smiled that same scary smile. And from the way he was fondling his shotgun, Gallagher figured that maybe he enjoyed his work a little too much.

CHAPTER SEVEN

There is an odor that accompanies death, an odor that humans cannot detect. But the creatures of the wood, those known and unknown to man, can. The smell wafts through the forest, alerting all to what has happened.

The insects are the first to be attracted. They eat and lay their eggs and thus continue their line. The ancients believed that it was the corpse that created the insects, that the sins of the body were released by death in the shapes of maggots and flies. This is mostly not true. However, on rare occasions, new life, different life does emerge, and new, unknown creatures enter the world.

Then come the scavengers, who feast on the flies, maggots, and dead flesh. Then the predators, who wait while the scavengers have their meal before pursuing and enjoying theirs.

Not all come. Some creatures prefer freshly killed meat to rotten flesh. Others sense the danger and stay away. And others are content to merely be aware.

Ama, the Snallygaster of York, was one such creature. Her mate having been struck down by lightning during a storm, she was content to lie in her cave, feed when she had to, and hope for a male to one day fly her way, a young one she hoped.

There were young ones to the south. She had sensed them on the wind: two females and two strong males. Ama had decided that when the time came, she would rest long, eat well, then send out her desire in hopes of attracting at least one. Two would be better. They could fight for her, and she would embrace the strongest and draw his life-making essence from him. Then perhaps when he was resting, she would use the other in the same way.

But it was not desire she now sensed in the wind. It was instead the presence of death that she had not experienced for some time. *Humans,* she realized. They passed through often, in the bellies of beasts that were not beasts. Rarely did they stop, and then only to rid themselves of waste, as all must do.

Despite the fading of the darkness and the coming of the light, Ama roused herself from her rest, left her cave, and, spreading her wings, took flight. As she flew, she was the death from above, the queen of the air. In the sky, the other night flyers gave way before her. On the ground, the creatures of the wood paid her obeisance, each in their way.

She found the bodies. When she appeared overhead, those near them backed away. When it became clear that she would not claim what was hers by right and might, they continued their feasting.

How? she sent by mind, scent, and sound so that all would understand.

Other humans, came the reply, *with the thunder that ends life.*

There was is no concept of "monster" among creatures. There were simply those to be feared, those to be eaten, and those to be avoided. But if there were, the Snallygaster of York might have thought, *What kind of monster kills its own kind?* As it was, she was merely confused.

Ama flew up. With the light about to chase away the dark, she sent out, *Humans killing humans in my domain.* Then specifically to the south, *How are your young?*

They kill their own here as well, came the reply from Kona, her southern cousin. Then in what can only be called an amused yet protective answer, *The fledglings are not yet old enough. You will have to wait.*

Having received the message, the Snallygasters of Bixby linked their minds.

Something might have to be done, Kona sent to Forra.

They hunt only others, not us.

And if they should?

They have tried before and failed. But should they try better, they are prey and easily caught, even if they do taste bad.

"The trucks didn't make it," Ricci told Sala once the others had reported in.

"What happened?" Sala asked from behind his desk, then indicated that Ricci could sit.

Ricci shook his head. "The decoy didn't notice they were missing until the truck behind him turned off on another road. Hard to say where it happened."

"Any word from our men?" Sala asked.

"The men driving the decoy went back to see if there was an accident but didn't find anything. No sign of the missing men either. Odds are Burke's men killed them. The York Road does cut through a heavily wooded area. If they were killed, it's likely they were hidden in the woods."

"Anything else?"

"One man said that when they went back he said he saw a, er, flying thing circling one area."

"What kind of 'flying thing'?"

"He called it a dragon, Mr. Sala."

Sala shook his head. "There are no dragons, not in this country anyway. It was likely a large bird flying low, a big owl maybe."

Sala decided not to mention snallygasters or any other such creatures. Some of his men were superstitious fools, likely to be cowards when it came to the unknown.

"Do you think it was Burke, Mr. Sala?"

Sala thought for a moment. "It is possible. No, it is likely. Regular hijackers do not kill. They only want the liquor. What they do not want is armed drivers fighting back. There is only one reason for our men to have been murdered." He paused to let Ricci figure it out for himself. Finally...

"Because our men would have recognized the hijackers?"

"Well done, Anthony."

Sala took the time to stand and pour them each a drink. Wine from Italy, imported long before the stupid law went into effect. *But*, Sala reflected as he handed Ricci his glass, *that stupid law will make us rich men.* "Now then," he asked, "what have you heard from the man we placed with Burke?"

"Nothing from Dylan, sir. I sent some people to his boarding house in Bixby. He's not there, and they don't know where he is."

"Then, Anthony, he was careless, and he paid the price for it. His death and the timing of it tells me that it was Burke who raided the trucks." He raised his glass. "Dylan, *che riposi in pace.*"

Che riposi in pace," Ricci echoed. After he had drunk, he asked, "Will you be reporting this to Mr. Martinelli?"

Letting out a long sigh, Sala said, "I do not think so. His response would be…excessive and involve everyone. It will attract attention we do not need. Let us do this. As was said, Burke was planning to bring in his goods around Westover. Send someone down there. Have him…no, send Maria Nigrone, they'd be likely to overlook a woman. Have her ask around about strangers, say she's looking for her brother or something like that, and report when it looks like Burke's trucks are about to leave. He owes us four trucks, so we will take his. After all, what is sauce for the goose is also sauce for the gander."

As the sun went down the night after the raid, the dwayyo gathered at the edge of the woods. There were three of them. There was Verr. There was Annarr, who might become leader should Verr weaken or leave the pack. And there was Naester, who might challenge Annarr for pack leader but would be beaten by her. They did not go into the open area, that was not for them, it was not their territory. But something had called them, and they had to answer.

It was a man, the man who had brought one of his own as food. That action had awakened primal memories, of a time when men honored the pack and left offerings. But that time was long gone.

The man stood where they could see him, where he could see them. At least, it looked like a man, smelled like a man, and wore the loose skin of a man that tasted bad. But its thoughts were not like men's. Its thoughts were dark and deep and were of things that the dwayyo understood. He was as much a predator as they were, a lone predator who followed a pack but was not one with the pack. Feeling this, Verr knew why this hunter had called to the pack. They alone understood him, and he, in his way, knew them.

In silent communion, the hunters stood there, until they all felt it was time to part. As Verr led Annarr and Naester away, he knew that this man who was not a man would again call, and they would answer, as if in answer to an even deeper primal memory.

When he saw what was happening, Duffy shouted for his boss.

"Paddy, come here, quick! Bring the Thompson."

Burke came on the run, machine gun in hand. "What is it?"

"Look."

They saw Jack standing there, the dwayyos closer than ever reported.

"Just what the Hell is going on? Are they going to attack or what? And why isn't the kid running? And where's his shotgun, I thought he was married to it."

"That he might be, Duff, but I don't think he needs it. They're the same kind, him and them." Burke thought of what Gallagher had told him about the hijacking, how the kid had been the one to start shooting. Burke decided not to do anything about it but rather wait and watch.

"One predator knows another, Duff. They must have seen Jack leave poor Dylan for them. I've heard they call to their prey, to freeze them just before attacking. They must have called to Jack."

"Why?"

"To thank him, to judge him, to see if it was a gift or a trap? Who knows the mind of such creatures? I guess right now they're taking each other's measure, maybe establishing boundaries. This far and no further will you go. I wouldn't be surprised if Jack pulled out his pecker and pissed a line to mark out his territory. Anyway, keep an eye on the boy. We may need him one day to protect us against the dwayyo. Make sure to tell the men, from now on Jack's gold. They are to protect him like one of their family. If they let him get killed, well, it would be better for them if they died as well."

The two left Jack outside with the dwayyo. How long he stood there, they didn't know. There was business to conduct. Sitting at a back table, they got a bottle of newly arrived rye whiskey and talked.

"Sala's probably gonna know it was us, what with Dylan 'going away' like that."

"He's not stupid, Duff. Of course, he knows it was us."

"Think he'll tell Martinelli? If he does, that might be the end."

"We're good, for now at least. If he does go running to Martinelli, it will go hard on us, but it will also be an admission that Sala can't handle his territory. Sala will then be removed, maybe permanently, and someone else put in his place. No, He'll keep quiet about what he knows. But he will be looking for payback."

"What'll he do, Paddy? Shoot up one of the houses? Take out some of the boys?"

"Not yet. Remember, he's just lost a lot of booze, and it's not like he can ask Martinelli for more. He'll be looking to replace it. I think he'll do me like I did him. When will we be ready to start shipping from Westover?"

"Still working with the locals, that sort of thing. First shipment in about a month."

"Let's make it two weeks. Send some trucks down. Hell, send down two of the trucks we took from Sala. Have whoever you send be obvious about it. I'm sure the dear, departed Dylan told Sala all about it anyway. Now then, who can we do without?"

"Gallagher told me that he thinks Johnson's on the needle, and Brown's been making noises that he thinks they all should be getting a piece of the action along with their pay."

"Who does he think he is, an organizer for the unions? Guess he hasn't heard what Bishop Quayle said about them. Send those two. Give them some dough for the trip down and tell them they'll be something special for them on the way back."

"Just the two of them, Paddy?"

Burke nodded, poured himself another drink, and topped off Duffy's glass. "Yeah, just those two. No sense risking more than that."

"So you think Sala's going hit us?"

"He has to, and we're gonna let him. What the hell, maybe he'll take it as a peace offering."

Chapter Eight

Once again, Marshal Russell Thorne went upstairs to his apartment a frustrated man. It was not because of the roadhouses. They had been relatively quiet. There had, of course, been the occasional fight between men who had had too much alcohol or threw around loud accusations of cheating in the gaming rooms, always by the losers. But the crew of the roadhouses had handled these competently and with the minimum force necessary. No one was so badly hurt in these incidents that they required hospitalization or even a doctor's care. And both Burke and Sala provided the marshal with full reports of each incident, in case there were questions later.

A few serious incidents did occur. One night Delilah West came into the Baxter House looking for her husband, Frank. She found him, and she found Betty, her second cousin, sitting on Frank's lap. Grabbing a bottle of the house rye, she first smashed it against her cousin's head then tried to use the jagged end of the bottle to remove a certain part of her husband's anatomy. She was disarmed before she could accomplish this, but Frank received a scar that would forever remind him of the virtues of fidelity.

Then one night, Henry Martin, who had come up from Harbor City to have a bit of fun at the Holden House, had had too much fun of the liquid kind. He smashed into a tree on the way home. Both he and his passenger, a lady to whom he was not related by either blood or marriage, were buried five days later.

Then there was the night of the big fight. Some of Martinelli's boys were celebrating at the Blair House, holding a bachelor sendoff for one of their crew who was getting married, when three couples walked in. One of these couples seemed very affectionate with each other. No one paid too much notice, that's what roadhouses were for after all, until the potential groom recognized the woman of the couple as his fiancé. That's when the fight started. At its height, everyone in the house was involved, including the bartenders and waitresses. When it was over, the injured were treated, the groom and his party paid for the damages, and the responding deputies took their reports. Surprisingly, the wedding went on as planned, the groom choosing to believe whatever story his bride told him.

It wasn't these things that frustrated Marshal Thorne. They were to be expected at a roadhouse. He was concerned at the level of cooperation that he received while investigating the cases, as if Sala and Burke were each planning something and were putting on a show of respectability, like little boys in December trying to behave, knowing that after Christmas they could drop the act and be themselves again.

Then again, Thorne thought one night out on his porch, *maybe those two are running a straight game and have nothing to hide. Yeah, and maybe one day I'll fly as high as whatever that thing is I keep seeing.*

No, what frustrated Russell Thorne was something that was going on in the towns. Although each town had its own sheriff, and those sheriffs their own deputies, enforcement of certain laws was lax at best. That they ignored drinking and gambling bothered Thorne, but he figured that they drank and gambled themselves, so they were not likely to take action unless it was so blatant they couldn't let it go. No, it was the doping and the doxies that bothered him. Victimless crimes some called it, but not so victimless for the women forced into the life, or the men who caught a disease and passed it on to their wives, or the people who got robbed so that some hophead could fill his needle.

It probably wasn't so bad before the roadhouses grew to more than a place to buy and drink 'shine and cider. But as they got bigger, so did the towns. The people who worked in the houses had to live somewhere, as did their families if they had any. In addition, people will want what they want, and where vice is denied in one place, it will pop up in another.

Should have planned for that, Russ, Thorne had told himself more than once.

He did what he could to fix things. The drugs were easy. Most of the townsfolk did not support it the way they did the local speaks. So when every arrested dope dealer wound up in the hospital for having "resisted apprehension," no one complained, and soon the hoppers had to drive into Harbor City to get fixed.

The cathouses were another story. People supported them, thought that they provided a service, believed that they kept "decent women" safe from the lusts and perversions of men. Russell Thorne was not one of those people. He tried to get a lead, but nobody, not even the town sheriffs, would talk to the marshal about them. His deputies were of no help, but Thorne had inherited them from Healy. With Thorn having cut off the "arrangement" money from the roadhouses, his deputies had to supplement their pay somehow, so they were probably being paid not to find out anything about the red-light cafes. So there was only one thing to do, Thorne decided, and that was to bring in an outsider to do the work of the Lord.

Dave's Place was a speakeasy on the Blair Road just inside northeast Harbor City. For the gangs that ran the city, Dave's was neutral ground. One could go there to meet with friends, to discuss serious matters with a rival, or to just have a quiet drink without the fear of someone pulling a gun on you.

Russell Thorne thought it a strange place for a lawman to meet, well, anyone. But the man he wanted to speak with insisted it was the only safe place in town.

No one noticed much when Thorne walked into Dave's Place. Some people turned to look at him, but to them, he was just another bimbo looking to get a drink or make a connection. Still, he felt vulnerable. He was sure that the Harbor City Police had warrants for half the men in the place and would like to question the other half.

Thorne had no problem finding the man he had come to see. Even sitting at a table against the far wall, Theodore Syn was easy to spot.

Thorne walked over to him and took the seat opposite. As he shook Syn's hand, he said, "Been a time, Scarecrow."

Tall with straw-yellow hair, Syn looked every bit his nickname. He didn't mind it. "Scarecrow" was a family name of sorts. Over 150 years ago, an English ancestor had used the name to cover his smuggling activity. But however much he looked like he should be standing in a field scaring away birds, Theodore Syn was more than that. He looked thin and maybe a bit slow, but there was quickness in his legs, strength in his arms, and a decent brain in his head. He had once been a cop in Baltimore but was fired after arresting a member of the City Council for murder.

"What was I supposed to do?" he had asked just before being dismissed, "He shot and killed a man in front of me."

"You should have dropped your cold piece on the ground and wrote it up as self-defense," explained his commanding officer.

"I don't carry a cold piece."

"That was your first mistake, Syn. Now get your belongings and get out before the mayor tells me to arrest you for assaulting the councilman."

After his dismissal, Syn made his way to Harbor City. Being a man with a brain and gun and the ability to use them both, he did well. Sometimes, he took jobs just because he needed the money. Other times, he helped people with no one else to turn to, for a price, of course. And if they didn't have the price, well, if he was flush, he helped them anyway.

"What can I do for you, Russ? Having too much fun in the sticks?"

"It's not been bad, Scarecrow, mostly quiet so far." Over their beers, Thorne told him of the gangs and how they might be building up to something big and nasty. Then he told him about his problems with the brothels.

"I need a man no one knows, a stranger."

Syn anticipated him. "You mean someone to go up to the bartender and say something like, 'I'm new to these parts. Where can I get a little action, and I don't mean liquor or poker'."

"Something like that."

"Might take a while."

"Take what time you need. I'll put you on the books as an anonymous special op, draw your pay myself and hand it over."

"They'll think you're fiddling."

Thorne shrugged. "So what? I'm a cop, it's expected."

Emptying and refilling their glasses, the two men sat, drank, and talked. Finally, Thorne asked, "You're from around these parts, aren't you?"

"Sort of. I'm from Frederick County. My father, Albert, was a tent preacher who worked a Western Maryland, Northern Virginia, and West Virginia circuit. And yes, by the time he passed, he had heard every joke there was about his last name. He even made up a few to use in his sermons. Da used to preach the gospel, bless the sick, and sell blessed elixir."

"Did it work?"

Syn shrugged. "Syrup and wine. Didn't do no harm, and it made people feel better. He also sold cigarettes made from what he called holy leaves."

"Let me guess. Muggles."

"Like I said, didn't do no harm, and it made people feel better. So what do you need to know about these parts?"

Thorne then described the flying thing he'd been seeing.

"You could have asked anyone. They'd have told you it's a snallygaster. There are nesting pairs all through these woods and mountains. Chances are there's dwayyo as well about."

Syn described both to the marshal. "Think of snallygasters as big birds that can eat you. If you stray into their hunting ground, just watch the sky and you might be all right. Think of dwayyo as nightmares come to life. They're pack animals. No, I think they're a step up from animals and a step below men. One of the Almighty's dead ends, you might say. Anyway, to the dwayyo, you're either pack or prey. You'll hear them before you see them, and if you see them, you better pray if they're after you, cause that will be the last thing you'll get to do."

"How about shooting them?"

"You might kill one, but that will only make the rest mad. Then they'll take a longer time eating you. Now the snallygasters, sometimes you can work with them."

"What do you mean, Scarecrow?"

Syn hesitated. *Shouldn't have said anything*, he thought. But he had brought it up.

"I'm not particularly proud of this, even though I hadn't even been born yet. Still, I guess somebody's got to tell the story."

⌇⌇⌇

My granddad, Josiah Syn, had what I guess you could call an affinity with the snallys. Said he could talk to them with his mind. He said it was because his da had married a woman from one of the Shawnee tribes.

My great grandad was Jeremiah Syn. Jeremiah was a man of the forest. He was always careful and respectful of the woods and the creatures that called it home. If there were dwayyo about, he managed to stay clear of them. And he knew enough not to be in a clearing at night when the snallygasters' shadows crossed the Moon.

One day, he was out hunting and checking his traps when he heard someone shout. It was a woman's voice, and it sounded like she was crying for help. Checking his gun, he ran toward where he had heard it.

It wasn't exactly a clearing, but there was enough space for four. Three of these were men, and one was a woman. From the way she was dressed, it looked as if she was part of one the Indian tribes us white men hadn't yet driven west.

What the men wanted was clear. They had torn her clothes and were trying to get her on her back so they could take turns. She was fighting them, but she was losing, so Jeremiah decided that she could use some help.

They managed to get her on the ground, and two of them held her while the third started undoing his pants. Jeremiah shot him, and he hit the ground before his pants did.

That got the attention of the others. It was a two-against-one fight. Knives were drawn, and blood flowed. Jeremiah stabbed one of the men in the leg artery and the other in the neck, but not before he took some deep cuts of his own. According to my da, who told me this story, Jeremiah told him that the last thing he remembered seeing before passing out was the Indian woman, who was scared and half-ready to run, but who stood there looking back at him. Jeremiah said that as things started to go black, he thought that at least he died doing a good thing.

Of course, he didn't die, or you would have been buying someone else a beer. Jeremiah woke up in the woman's village. She said her people were part of the Piscataway tribe. He was bandaged and on the mend. He had saved her, and now she had saved him.

Well, him being a man and she being a woman, one thing led to another. The tribe was small, so no one had any objection to new blood being introduced into it, least of all the woman. Jeremiah never did tell us her tribal name; he always called her Alice. So they got married according to the tribal way, and when the tribe moved on, Alice stayed with Jeremiah, and they raised a family.

Alice had been the tribe's medicine woman or shaman or something like that. My grandad said that her magic was in his blood, and that's why he could talk to the snallygasters.

Now, this is the part I'm not proud of. Every family has one or two, some have more, and for some families, it would have been better if their long-ago ancestors had never met and so saved the world all the trouble they caused.

Josiah Syn was the one in our family, the one who lived up to how our name was pronounced. He was a liar, a cheat, a braggart, and a bully. This was before the Civil War, and to put food on the table, Josiah became a hunter of men. Of course, he didn't see it that way. To him, he was in the business of recovering property, that property being runaway slaves. He worked the forests and the deep woods, and those who went on hunts with him said that he was always accompanied by a great flying beast.

My da heard him talking about it one night.

"I was out in the dark forest, looking for this one runaway. The daylight was fading, and I knew if it got dark I'd never find him, what with his black skin and all. I came across this cave, and there it was. I had never before seen a snallygaster, but I knew what it was, and I knew I was dead. As it came toward me, I thought, *Dear God, no, stop,* and to my surprise, it did. I then re-membered how my mother could get dogs and cats and other beasts to do what she wanted. Since I was her blood, I tried it with the snally. It fought me, but my mind was stronger, and soon it would do whatever I wanted. I sent it an image of the one I was hunting, and it flew off. Soon it came back with the slave. But damn if he wasn't dead and half-eaten. But we worked on that, and soon it was bringing them back alive."

Since storytelling is thirsty work, Thorne got each of them another beer. At least, he got Syn another one. He had barely touched his second. "So your grandfather used snallygasters to hunt slaves?" he asked.

"Yeah."

"Not your sin, Scarecrow, if you'll pardon the expression. What happened to him?"

Syn shrugged. "No one knows. One day he didn't come home. And that was all right. Nobody cared. Nobody missed him."

Syn finished his story thinking, *Not quite the truth but close enough for Jazz. I don't think Russell would believe what really happened. Can't say I believe it myself.*

"So, are you going to help me or not?" Thorne asked when he and Syn walked out to their vehicles.

"Why the hell not? And once you close down enough of these houses of ill repute, maybe I can be one of your deputies? It would be nice to be a lawman again."

CHAPTER NINE

Johnson and Brown's trip to Westover was uneventful. No one expected otherwise. There's no profit in hijacking empty trucks. When they got near to the city, they had trouble finding exactly where it was they were supposed to go.

"Can't make out these directions," Peter Brown said. "Can you, Bobby?"

Bobby Johnson looked at the piece of paper. For him, the ride down had been too long. He was hurting for a fix. He had one before he left, and now he could not wait to get to a room and ride the juice. Two shots a day was all he needed, well, maybe one just before bed to help with the dreams. In the morning, another one should last him until he got back to Bixby. He hoped so, if anything happened to the shipment, if he ran off the road or something, Burke would kill him, assuming he survived the crash.

Johnson looked at the paper Brown had handed him. He could read a little better than Brown. He worked out where to go, it was east of some kind of plantation, and soon the two trucks were heading in that direction, neither man noticing the small, black coupe that started following them when they neared the plantation.

It can't be this easy, Maria Nigrone said to herself. She'd been in and around Westover for a week now, letting hopeful men buy her drinks and asking after her "brother" who had written her that he was coming up from Mexico on a ship. She'd had to endure pawing, groping, and one near assault that left her would-be assailant with a broken arm and a permanent facial scar. She'd turned down offers from men to "show her some good times" and "get her in good with the clubs up in Richmond." Other offers involved straight financial transactions. This she understood, having briefly lived that life before a young man named Anthony recognized her potential and introduced her to Vincent Sala. Neither man demanded the usual from her, Anthony because he wasn't interested and Sala because, as he put it when they first met, "Anthony was right, *signora*. You are beautiful. If only I were not married and you were not working for me."

Soon she got word of a small boat that had brought a shipment up the James River that was unloaded at a farm just east of the Westover Plantation.

Maria had already been to the plantation and had made some arrangements for both of the men she worked for.

When Brown and Johnson arrived, they were directed to pull into a barn. Once inside, they asked a man named Greenwood if they could wash up and get something to eat, and maybe grab a nap.

"I'm afraid not, fellas," Greenwood said, pulling a pistol from his waistband.

Brown took a quick look behind him. Two more men, two more guns. Brown said, "It's like that, huh?"

Greenwood nodded. "Yeah, it's like that."

The two men were made to face the wall. "Sorry about this, guys," Greenwood said, "but it's orders. You got one minute to make your peace with the Creator."

Johnson understood. He was sure Brown did too. It was part of the life they had chosen. In his last few seconds, Johnson felt the urge start to grow inside him, and his last thought before the thunder of the guns was, *At least its ov...*

Maria had stopped just outside the plantation grounds. She waited until she heard two faint gunshots, then she returned to Westover. She had a few calls to make. Once this was done, her job was over. She'd leave the next morning for Richmond. There she'd meet a man, a rich man, a handsome man with brown eyes and a nice smile. He had been a client when she was on the game, and after she left that life, she had kept in touch with him. He had written in his letters that he cared little for the past and looked forward only to a future with her. Maria would have liked that, liked it very much. What a shame that not too long ago he had crossed a man named Martinelli and that this Martinelli was paying to have him killed. Maria had decided to give this man a wonderful night before sending him to God. *Too bad*, she thought, *but there were other brown-eyed handsome men, and just maybe I won't have to kill the next one I meet.*

Now driven by different men, the trucks went on, following the same route they had taken on the trip south. None of the men inside the trucks knew what they were carrying. They probably thought they did, but they hadn't watched the trucks being loaded. By not knowing what their cargo was, if stopped by troopers or treasury agents, they could somewhat honestly argue their innocence. Not that anyone would believe them, but it would give a paid-off judge an excuse to let them go with a warning.

As they neared the end of their journey, they bypassed Bixby and went north to just outside Blair. Once there, they drove the trucks into an old barn to be unloaded.

There was room for both trucks in the barn. Men gathered to help the drivers unload. The back latches were released, and the rear doors opened, thus triggering the bombs inside both trucks.

The twin explosions destroyed the barn and killed the men inside it. Trees were uprooted, and the windows of the roadhouse kitchen shattered, the flying glass badly cutting the people inside. Frightened by the unknown noise, shaken by the shockwaves that hit them, the creatures of the dark woods fled.

Echoes of the blasts were heard as far south as Bixby. On hearing and feeling them, the dwayyo would have run toward them but for their leader. Associating the distant sound with the thunder made by men, Verr told his pack, *This is not for us. It is man's business, not ours.*

In their nest, the Snallygasters heard the blasts as well. They felt the thoughts of the dying and of the frightened prey that would be running their way. But they had fed well that night.

Leave them, there will always be prey, Kona sent as she tended to her hatchlings.

Yes, Forra agreed and went outside to stand guard until it was her turn to fly high and enjoy the night while he covered the young to keep them warm.

Theodore Syn had completed his job of locating the brothels throughout Corbett County. Posing as a passing stranger, he had talked to bartenders and patrons of the various roadhouses. He found that there were one or two of the houses in each town, and some set up in cabins conveniently located near the roadhouses.

"We'll hit them first," Russell Thorne said after Syn had made his report. The two were in the marshal's apartment, Thorne drinking coffee; Syn, Coca-Cola. With his apartment on the third floor of the marshal's office, Thorne said it would set a bad example if he kept any alcohol there.

"Are you sure you want to shut them down, Russ?" Syn asked as they moved the discussion outside to Thorne's balcony.

"Why do you ask?"

"Well, to be honest, I think shutting down these houses would be a lot like Prohibition. People want what they want, and they'll get it any way they can. Why not regulate these red-light cafés? Make sure the girls are healthy and being treated good and that none of them are there against their will?"

Thorne shook his head. "Drinking is one thing, Scarecrow, this is something different. Sex outside marriage is a sin, but it happens and may be forgiven. But sex for money, that's a worse sin, and it taints all those involved—the men, the women, and those who profit by it. I can't abide it, and as marshal and a God-fearing man, I can't permit it."

"So you get to decide what sins people can commit, is that it?"

Whatever response Thorne might have made was stopped by a muffled boom coming from the north. Neither man thought it was thunder.

"I know that sound," Thorne said. "Heard it enough in the Great War."

"Same here."

For a moment, both men fought back memories of artillery barrages and men dying in trenches.

"Might be you got another war starting up," Syn suggested.

"I think you mean 'we,' Deputy Syn?"

"It's about time you offered. I guess I'll have to call you 'Marshal' and wear a uniform."

"You'll get a uniform, it comes with the badge, but you'll be of better use to me if you don't wear it."

"So, I'd be a detective?" Thorne nodded. "How much does it pay?"

"Not enough, and the hours are lousy."

"Sounds like fun." Syn then pointed in the direction from which the explosion had come. "What are you going to about that?"

"For tonight, Scarecrow, hope and pray that nothing catches fire and, if so, the fire doesn't spread. Tomorrow I'll go see what blew up."

"And if it's the start of a war?"

"The war has already started." Thorne thought about bodies on the York Road, and trucks seen driving south into Virginia, and how a man named Dylan had disappeared and the rumors about why he had. "As long as the right ones die and civilians aren't involved, I'm gonna let Burke and Sala fight it. When it's over, we can bury the losers and hang the winners."

"Russ, we both know there are no winners in a war, just one side that loses less than the other. What kind of lawman are you?"

"You said it yourself, Scarecrow, I'm the kind that decides what sins people can commit, and how to punish them when they do."

Russell Thorne walked slowly around where a barn used to be. He then inspected the area surrounding the barn, looking to see how far the debris had spread, keeping in mind that there had been two bombs, one in each of the trucks that were now nothing more than twisted metal. He was no expert, but the diameter of the circles told him that it had been a fairly large blast. He knew that there were scientists who could probably tell him what kind of explosive was used and exactly how much, but they were down in Washington, and he had no intention of calling them in.

He looked over from where the barn used to be to the back of the Blair House. It was undamaged. The Blair had a separate kitchen, and that protected it. Thorne was wondering if that was a good thing or not when a car pulled up. A chauffeur emerged. He opened the back door and Vincent Sala got out, closely followed by his assistant, Anthony Ricci. "Marshal Thorne, what are you doing here?"

"Good morning, Mr. Sala. I've been expecting you. I have a few questions. But as to your question," Thorne looked away from the man, toward the barn, then back again, "something blew up. I'm the marshal. It's my job to investigate."

"Marshal, you are on private property, my property, legally leased from the county. I must ask you to leave until you have the proper, written authority."

Unspoken were the words, "And good luck getting that." And that was true, Sala might not own any judges, but quite a few could be rented for an hour or two.

Just like the girls in red-light cafés, Thorne thought and wondered if he was going after the wrong people.

Thorne had dealt with men like Sala before, petty kings of minor kingdoms. He had not been impressed by them, and he was not impressed by Sala.

"Mr. Sala," he said calmly but with an edge in his voice. "Last night, two trucks were blown up and men died." Sala tried to interrupt, but Thorne went on. "Your people tried to clean things up by removing the bodies, but it was dark, and they did not do a very good job. As I look around, I can see pieces of them splattered all over. That makes this area a crime scene, and as such, it's my property until I say it isn't." Thornes' voice got harsher, his eyes meaner. "Of course, I could shut you down, here and in Holden in case there's any evidence there, until I get 'the proper, written authority,' and that might take me a week or so. So what's it gonna be?"

Vincent Sala was a man used to giving orders. He was not used to being defied by anyone, especially someone who wore a badge. He had bought so many men with badges that he was contemptuous of the whole lot. But he was also a man who knew when to yield when circumstances demanded it.

"Marshal, why don't we go inside and discuss things?"

To Thorne, there was always something strange about a bar, a speak, or a roadhouse when it was closed. It was as if it were asleep and would not be awake until the sun set and people came to fill it.

"I would offer you something to drink, Marshal, but I do not think you would accept."

"You are right, Mr. Sala, I would not. But, given the circumstances, if you need a little something, I would not object."

To take a drink then would be a sign of weakness, so Sala went without as well.

"Mr. Sala, let's not kid each other. Your barn, your trucks, your men, your problem. Those trucks were supposed to be running illegal alcohol and instead brought back bombs. I've told you before, right now, I don't give care about Prohibition or the act that supports it. That's for the Treasury boys to worry about. What I do care about is that people got killed. Now either you brought back the bombs to use against someone else, or someone planted them in your trucks and set them off to hurt you. Which is it?"

"Marshal, if I were the kind of man who would be cowardly enough to use indiscriminate weapons like explosives against an opponent, I would not be foolish enough to store them on my property. As for who would want to cause me harm, you just have to look south of the city."

"Burke?"

"You have said it, Marshal, not I."

Just then, there was a commotion outside, shouts of "Stop" and "You can't go in there." Marshal loosened his revolver in its holster. He was prepared to draw when Patrick Burke entered the roadhouse.

"Sala," he shouted, "I'm glad to see you alive. Marshal, I called your office and was told you were here and had to come. Someone's trying to kill me."

Uninvited, Burke sat at the table with the two men. Sala offered a drink and Burke took a drop of the good stuff. With Burke drinking, Sala felt that he could as well. Thorne pretended not to notice.

"Tell me about it, Mr. Burke."

"It's like this, Marshal. I had arranged for certain goods to be shipped from Mexico to, well, somewhere in Virginia. I think that my shipment was switched for the bombs that I've heard went off last night. It's well-known that I inspect every shipment I receive. These bombs were meant for me."

"And why is it that the trucks with the bombs reached me and not you?" Sala asked before Thorne could.

"I think my trucks were hijacked along the way. It happens all the time. The drivers were probably killed since I haven't heard from them. As to how they ended up with you, maybe you know because I don't. Maybe someone's out to get us both. Present company excepted, Marshal."

Thorne had heard enough. "Burke, I'll want your contacts in Virginia. Sala, I'll need you to produce the bodies for a coroner's examination, along with the names of any men that can't be accounted for. Good day, gentlemen."

Well, Thorne thought as he drove back to Dunkirk. *I've done my job and investigated the explosion. Things are in motion. Let's see what happens next.*

Chapter Ten

Vincent Sala called a meeting as soon as he was back in his offices in Holden. In addition to himself and Ricci, there were Dale Fontana and Andrew Rossi, managers of the Holden and Blair Houses, as well as Nicholas Costello, who had no specific title but was known to be a man who could get things done with no questions, no hesitation, and no remorse.

"It was Burke behind the bomb that killed my men and almost destroyed my roadhouse," Rossi said. "He knew we were gonna hijack him, so he set the whole thing up."

"Of course, it was Burke." Sala's voice barely rose above his normal tone, but still, it managed to convey a sense of outrage at Burke's actions and impatience with Rossi for stating the obvious. "He declared war when he hit our trucks and killed our men. And, anticipating what our response would be, he set a trap for us. A dangerous trap for it might have gone wrong in so many ways. Now he waits to see what we will do. If we do nothing, then we, no, *I* will appear weak."

"But if we strike back," Costello said, "the marshal will know it was us and take action."

Sala shook his head. "I do not think so. I do not think Marshal Thorne cares. He knows the roadhouses are here to stay, even after Prohibition is repealed. He will let us fight and deal with whoever wins. I plan to be the man he deals with." He looked at Costello. "Nicholas, I think a controlled response is in order, but one that sends the right message. Tonight, or rather, tomorrow morning after it has closed, take some of your men and make the

Lambert House go away. Burn it or blow it up, I don't care, but make sure it's gone. Try to keep injuries and fatalities to a minimum. Tomorrow, I will call Burke to discuss peace. There is enough to go around for all of us, for now. Later, when Burke has begun to relax, only then will we take all that he has and leave him a broken man."

"Both Thorne and Burke are going to know we were behind the Lambert."

Sala shook his head in correction. "No, Anthony, they will suspect but will not be able to prove anything. Who knows, maybe Burke was right when he suggested that we had a mutual enemy. Which is another reason for a truce between us."

Patrick Burke was feeling good after his visit with Sala and the marshal. They both thought he was responsible, but there wasn't a damned thing they or he could do about it. Thorne didn't seem to care one way or the other. Burke knew his game and was determined to be the only other one playing in the end.

Burke knew that Sala was going to hit back. He had to. It was either that or go back to wherever the hell he had come from. He'd hit one of the houses, probably soon.

Sala wouldn't be fool enough to attack when they're open, Burke thought. *Not unless he has some men just drive by and fire a few shots to scare away the customers. Thorne wouldn't stand for anything more than that. No, Sala will hit either before or after. I better post men all around.*

When he got back to Bixby, he called Jack Reilly in for a quiet meeting, just the two of them.

"Jackie," he said. "I'm gonna need you the next few nights, really need you. Sala's men are gonna attack, maybe tonight, maybe in the next few nights."

"Do you want me to kill him for you, Mr. Burke?" The young man asked calmly, with no more expression than if asking Burke if he wanted a drink.

Now there's an idea. In his mind, Burke thought about what he'd say to the police. *"The boy must have overheard me talking about*

Sala, about how I'd love it if he were gone. Jack, well, he's a good lad but not too bright. He must have taken it into his head to make Sala gone."

Yes, that might work, Burke thought, *if all else fails. After all, what's the good of a weapon if you don't use it?*

But to Jack, he said, "No, my boy, that's not how it's done. What I need from you is to take charge of the guards around the house, from before closing until the sun rises. Anyone who comes on the property is to be stopped and challenged. Anyone who won't stop, well, make sure they are stopped, however you have to. Unless it's the Marshal or his deputy, of course. Once we open, you can stand down but be ready for trouble."

Don't worry, Mr. Burke, I'll do everything I can. And if they do attack," the boy smiled in anticipation, "I'll take as many as I can with me."

"I know you will, Jackie. I know you will?"

"Is there, uh, anything else, Mr. Burke?"

The way Jack asked this made Burke think that he was expecting something more. "Not now, Jack. If there is, I'll let you know."

Despite the guards, the crews at all of Burke's roadhouses were nervous. They knew what had happened, knew what was probably going to happen, but they trusted Burke to keep them safe, trusted that the extra men he had in place around each establishment would protect them.

Everything was in place. The guards outside the building on Lambert Road stood ready. They were armed with Thompson machine guns and pump-action shotguns. There were patrols and fixed positions. Any attempt to assault the roadhouse would be repulsed, and the attackers killed, and the best part was that it would all be in self-defense. They were ready for anything.

Or so they thought.

Some men who had fought in the Great War could not adjust to the quiet life of peacetime. Some joined police departments, some waged their own private wars on crime. Still others returned overseas to fight in other countries' wars for whichever side paid the most. And others were sought after by organizations like Sala's.

The men who were guarding the Lambert House were not these kinds of men. Most of them had remained behind and let other men fight and die for their country. They were not prepared for the men who attacked that night.

As the time for opening came, those inside the Lambert waited for the diners, drinkers, and gamblers to arrive. As long as the customers were there, everyone was safe. Only treasury men raided open establishments, and they only did that when they needed to make it look like they were doing their jobs.

The servers, waitresses, bartenders, and musicians did not know that just after sunset, the Lambert Road had been closed in both directions. As they started wondering where their customers were, the shooting started.

Sharpshooters who had honed their skills in French trenches took out the guards who had thought Tommys and shotguns were enough. As they fell, armed men who were standing by attacked. Smashing open doors, they entered firing.

The guards that had been stationed within fired back, and there was blood and death on both sides. But the invading force was better prepared and better trained. Some of those inside tried to flee through the kitchen to no avail. The attackers who were placed in the rear took great delight in picking them off one by one as they sought to escape. Soon all was quiet except for the occasional gunshots that ensured there would be no survivors.

When Lambert Road finally opened, those driving to the roadhouse, the ones who had not turned around at the sound of not so distant gunfire, took one look at the bodies outside and the fires that had been started inside and continued on. No one thought to stop to help. No one drove into town to notify the police. They did not want to get involved. It was not their problem.

Ironically, the slaughter was discovered by the men Sala had sent to destroy the Lambert. Their job having been done for them, they left. There was some debate as to whether or not to blow up the Baxter, but in the end, they decided to call the Lambert sheriff's office. The sheriff, deciding that the road to Lambert was not Lambert itself, passed the information to the County Marshal's office.

That night, the night before the dead at the Lambert were discovered, Jack Reilly was making one last circuit. He was tired and looking forward to sleep. He was also disappointed that no one had attacked the Bixby.

"Sean."

It was the whispered voice he had expected earlier.

"What is it?'

"Something's happened. You'll hear about it soon. Paddy needs you to do something very important for him."

"What is it?"

"Those dwayyo you talk to. Can you get them to do what you want?"

"It's not like that. It's not like talking, not the way you and me do. The pack and me, we sort of understand each other. That's all."

"Would they understand you if you warned them of danger?"

"They might, if they had reason to."

"Good. Here's what you'll need to do."

By mid-morning of the next day, Russell Thorne, his deputies, and Theodore Syn were looking at what remained of the Lambert House. After commandeering enough trucks to take the bodies to St. Anlee's hospital in Dunkirk, they were left with the arduous (and ultimately useless task) of gathering evidence.

"Tell me, *Marshal*, is this one of those sins you've decided to allow, or are you going to take some action against who did this?"

Choosing to ignore his newly appointed detective's sarcasm, Thorne said, "Knowing who did it and proving it are two differ-ent things, *Detective*. Now we can pull bullets and pellets out of here and out of the bodies in the hospital's morgue. And there are some police scientists who can tell from them what kinds of guns were used, and a few who are working on matching bullets to each other and to the guns that fired them. They'd be interested in those bullets. But they're not here, and if they were, there are no guns to compare them to. And unless that magic Indian blood your slave-hunting grandfather may have passed down to you allows you to talk to the dead, we don't have any witnesses. So, what exactly am I supposed to do?"

"Shut them down. Close the roadhouses and allow tempers to cool. Last I heard, serving alcohol and allowing gambling is against the law. Maybe it's time to enforce that."

As his men waded through the blood and picked through the debris, gathering left-behind personal effects and spent ammunition, Thorne thought about what Syn had said.

"I could seize and smash their liquor and padlock their doors, but a local judge would only fine them and order me to let them open up again. They'd be back in business, and this," he indicated the crime scene, "will happen again, and again. Best to let them fight it out now and get it all over with. They'll all be gone in a week."

"You know, Russ, I'm beginning to think those fellows in black may just have the right idea."

Thorne laughed. "They mean well, but like us, they can only slow the crooks down. Thanks to Prohibition, criminals are starting to organize. Once they do, they'll be with us forever."

"You can't change the world, Marshal."

"No, Scarecrow, but I can push back against the evil around me."

In his room on the second floor of the Bixby Roadhouse, Jack Reilly could not sleep. He had heard about what had happened the previous night, about the raid on the Lambert Roadhouse. He was angry but not for what had been done, for that was the way of things. Kill or be killed. Eat or be eaten. It was the way of those like him.

Like him, not like his father. His father did not stay to fight. His da ran and wanted him to run as well. Jack ran, but only away from his old life.

Jack thought back to when he was still Sean Meadows. He remembered being happy, playing with sisters, hunting and 'shining with his da and brother. He would still be happy if it had not been for that night in the woods.

He did not see what his father had called the dway that night. He saw their shadows and felt their hunger and power. They had wanted him not to fight, wanted him to be afraid. Instead, he was ready to fight and die, and he found himself happy and excited by the idea.

No, Jack Reilly was not mad that men he had known and worked with had been killed. He was mad because he had not been there. To fight and possibly die, and in dying, take others with him. That was what he needed. He was a hunter, and he needed prey. He had expected more when he left Baltimore to join with Burke. But other than that night on the York Road, the night when he had the power and he caused the fear, there had been nothing.

Nothing but dwayyo, nothing but the pack.

Even as he thought of them, he heard their call. Never before had they called to him. It was he who stood near the woods and called to them. Could this be why he could not sleep that tonight?

Getting out of bed, he got dressed. Given what had happened that night, he took up his shotgun, loaded it, and went out to answer the call.

He had to be careful. He could not think of what he had been asked him to do. He did not want to do it, but Burke was his boss, his leader, and, like the pack, he would follow his leader.

Think only of truths, he told himself as he approached the leader and his two.

When he saw them at the edge of the woods, he placed his shotgun on the ground. He did not need it against the dwayyo, but there were others, and this night of all nights, he wanted it near him. He opened his thoughts and, for the first time, heard the dwayyo pack leader in his mind.

Your kind kills its own. Why? It is not for food.

We are not one pack but many. Many packs fight to lead all.

Then why do not your leaders fight? Why waste the members of the pack and cause them to leave it? We have always wondered this.

Jack answered truthfully. *I do not know. It is our way.*

A nasty thought was the leader's reply. It was something about an animal who voids on another's food. It implied that man's way was worse than this.

It was time to do what Burke's man had told him.

Have you pack members who go mad, who become something that is a danger to the rest? Jack asked.

Yes, Verr replied. *There is sickness of the body and sickness of the mind. The body sometimes heals; if not, it leaves the pack. The mind once sick may heal, or it may not. If it does not, if something like the white foam or the fear of water comes upon one, if it snaps and bites another of the pack and it is not a challenge or our mating season, that one is driven out. If it returns...it is the only time that the pack may destroy its own.*

The ones who fought last night, Jack sent, *the ones who used the thunder on the other packs of men, they have this sickness. My leader has tried to send them away, but they will not leave, and so will be a danger to our other packs and maybe to yours.*

He sent a thought of what Tommys and shotguns could do to the pack, of how they would be hunted once these maddened killers finished with their own.

We will go deep, the leader sent, *away from your maddened packs.*

They will go deeper, after you, Jack thought back. *I can help you destroy them, and so your pack will be safe.* Then, just as Burke had told it to him, he told them how and when.

We will call, came the answer, *or we will not. If we do not, we have gone deep.*

Then Verr, Annarr, and Naester faded back into the shadows and were gone. Jack turned and picked up his shotgun. On his way to his room, he searched his mind for any sense of guilt or betrayal. Of guilt, he had none. He was merely doing what he had been told to do. He did not want to think about betrayal. He had, in a way, formed a bond with the dwayyo. He was, in a way, somewhat like them. But he knew he was possibly leading them to their deaths. *Possibly my death as well*, he thought, *for I'll be leading them*. And who knows? Maybe people will become so afraid that they will leave the dwayyo alone. Even knowing that it was the nature of humans to kill what they feared, somehow Jack Reilly convinced himself that this was the best for all.

What shall be done? Verr asked his two strongest as they neared the packhome. They had listened to his communication with the man who was not quite a man.

A beast that kills its own is a danger to all beasts, said Annarr, the first of his two.

We are not all beasts, and we are a danger to men, Naester said.

We are a danger to some men, when they are but a few. Together, they are many more than our pack, Verr argued.

But to hunt us, they must enter our ground where they may not stand together, and so we can hunt them, countered Annarr.

To this, Naester said, *At night, when the Moon shines, or it does not, we can hunt them. But they hunt by day as well. What if they seek out the packhome and the young ones?*

Enough! The force of their leader's thought silenced them. He had taken their counsel and made his decision.

When the one who is not a man calls, the pack will gather in the darkness at the edge of our ground. We will send our thoughts to these maddened men, slowing and confusing them.

Indicating Annarr, he sent, *You will take three of the young ones and hunt man on his own ground. What will then happen will happen. If we do well, then we will continue the hunt. But if we must, we will go deep into the woods, but we will go after a fight and a feast.*

What of the flying ones if we go deep? Naester asked.

The flying ones can stay on the high ground, answered Verr. *If they come for us, then we will go after them.*

CHAPTER ELEVEN

The investigation into the Lambert massacre took all day and went on until the coming of night made it too dark to work. As he returned to his boarding house in Dunkirk, Theodore Syn was disturbed. Partly by what he had seen at the Lambert, but he had seen worse in France, when men could not get to their masks in time when the bombs fell. Or when they were cut down trying to advance another few hundred feet. *That was war*, he told himself even as he realized that this, too, was war, only a different kind. But it was a war in which people died not for their country but over drinking and gambling and who gets to provide it.

What had happened at the Lambert and at the Blair made no sense. The level of violence, which could only increase, was of the type that sooner or later the governor would have to take notice.

Sala and Burke had to know this, had to know that the game they played all but assured their mutual destruction. If things went on as they were, the governor would call in the State Police and the militia, and possibly get the Federal government involved. Everything would then be shut down. Maybe there was nothing that could be done against the gangs in Chicago, Detroit, and Harbor City, but five...make that *four* roadhouses out in the nowhere were easy targets, and it would make it look as if someone were actually doing something.

So why were they doing it? Maybe they were both mad, so caught up in vengeance that they didn't care.

Russ didn't seem to care either. Maybe that's what he was planning. Let it get bad enough so that action had to be taken, even if it does cost a few lives. Syn thought about what he knew about his friend. Back in Coast City, Russell Thorne was not averse to life-taking when he thought it was needed. But that was more direct action.

A terrible idea suddenly came to the Scarecrow. He could not believe it, but it did explain what was happening. Why the level of violence had gone beyond hijackings and had bypassed the quiet murders that are the usual strategy of this kind of war. Maybe Sala and Burke were not mad, but someone who hated them and what they were doing was. He could only think of one person, and the thought frightened him. And what he might have to do to make things right frightened him even more.

Once back in Dunkirk, Syn parked on the lot that Mrs. Taylor provided for the residents of her boarding house. As he walked around to the front to let himself in—as a lawman, he had key privileges—he heard in the distance the familiar sound of a train whistle and knew it for what it really was. It reminded him of the story he had told Thorne and of the truth behind that story.

With the bath and shower room empty this time of the evening, Syn took a long wash and then returned to his room. From his bookcase, he removed a battered diary written by his great-grandmother in the neat, precise English she had learned after she had married his great-grandfather Jeremiah. Sitting down, he turned to the back and began to read.

The great Sky Beast called to me last night. She came into my thoughts as she had into my mother's and her mother's, as all the Sky Beasts have with the wise women of my tribe.

The Sky Beasts protected us, kept us from harm, made sure that the Hairy Beasts knew that we were not their prey, that the Sky Beasts watched over us. There was, for this, a cost, as there is for all things.

There are and always have been few Sky Beasts. At times, their blood runs thin and the eggs the female hatches do not produce chicks or the chicks do not survive. New blood is needed, new essence to renew their line. The Sky Beasts care not from whom this essence is obtained, only that is it given willingly, and that it comes from a male.

This is the price, and I have been asked to provide it.

When I told Jeremiah of the Sky Beast's request, he asked if it would hurt. I did not know for that was something of which we did not speak. He wanted to know if it would kill him. I told him that only a few of the men who went to the Sky Beast's embrace failed to return, but that all who did were in some way changed. Just how I could not tell him, for that was another thing of which we did not speak.

Then he asked, "Will you be with me?" When I said that I would be, then and always, he said, "What the hell? I've always wanted to see a snallygaster."

The next night when the moon shone bright, we ascended to her cave. If she had a mate, he was not there, nor did we see his shadow in the sky. When she emerged from the cave, I thought Jeremiah would run. Her wings folded, she stood on two legs, the tentacles which covered her mouth waving as tree limbs do in a gentle wind. She was both beautiful and frightening in her aspect, and from her mind came thoughts of safety and gratitude.

Let us begin.

Jeremiah removed his clothes and approached her. Slowly and gently, she wrapped her tentacles around him. Her wings unfurled, and as she lifted him into the sky, he uttered a cry of mixed pain and pleasure.

How long they flew, I do not know. It seemed both forever and no time at all. When they landed, and she released him, Jeremiah was weak and pale but otherwise unharmed.

Let him rest, *I heard in my mind.* When you depart, he may forever walk in the deep wood undisturbed, for the mark is upon him. *As she disappeared into her cave, she added,* Thank you, both of you.

We spent the night outside the cave. In the morning, Jeremiah was strong enough to leave.

After his experience with what he called a snallygaster, Jeremiah was a changed man. The vigor he had had in his youth returned, and for many nights after, it was as if we were newly married. The marks her tentacles left on his body never did fade.

How could I explain that to Russell? Syn thought as he closed his great-grandmother's diary. That it was not her Indian blood that allowed Josiah to command the snallygaster but rather his father's essence in the sky beast.

And I have some of that essence, Syn thought. *I wonder…*

But Theodore Syn had more important things to worry and wonder about, so after replacing the diary, he turned off his light and went to sleep.

The following morning, Burke and Sala both received "invitations" from Marshal Thorne to accompany his deputies to the Dunkirk House. The Dunkirk was neutral ground, owned and run by a somewhat smallish fellow named Moran who served beer, wine, and whiskey in good measure and at a fair price. He did not offer food, gambling, music, or any other kind of entertainment, the Dunkirk was just a place to have a quiet drink either alone or with friends.

At the request of Thorne, Moran had opened early, just past lunch, but only for the Marshal's guests. Moran offered them coffee, juice and, soft cider but none of the hard stuff. For all that he protected Moran, Thorne was the law, and to do otherwise would be disrespectful.

Burke and Sala had not been permitted to bring anyone with them. Thorne brought Theodore Syn as well as the deputies who had escorted the gang leaders. Syn was in plain clothes and stayed apart from the group, leaving Burke and Sala to wonder just why he was there.

Once they had been seated and served, Sala and Burke each began to complain about their treatment and to protest both their innocence and their arrest. Thorne let them talk themselves out, and when they quieted…

"Okay, you two. Let's review. Burke, were you involved in blowing up trucks and people at the Blair House?"

"I've told you before, Marshal, I think I was the target, and I want to know…"

"You've sung that song before, Burke. A yes or no will do."

"No."

"And you, Sala, were you responsible for what happened at the Lambert House last night?"

Sala was about to give a long answer, but at the look Thorne gave him, he said merely, "No, Marshal."

"Then why was your man Costello seen near there both before and after?"

"Why you..." Burke rose up. If the table had not been between them, he would have gone for Sala. One push from Thorne and Burke sat down hard.

"Let him answer," the marshal said.

Sala thought carefully, then spoke.

"I will confess, Marshal, Burke, to having instructed Costello to do something in retaliation for what happened at Blair. Property damage, yes. Loss of life, hopefully not. To this end, Costello was to wait until after closing to make his move. The tragic assault on the Lambert House was not his doing, nor was it mine. And before you ask, Marshal, Costello did not recognize any of the attackers."

After listening from his post at the bar, Syn thought, *Interesting how Russ knew about Costello. Does he have a man on the inside, or did he have a watcher in the woods? Or maybe he was there, watching for himself?*

Thorne's voice interrupted his thoughts.

"Here's how it's gonna be, you two. As we speak, I've got men hitting the cafés you have in town. And don't bother denying they're yours. If they're not, then no harm to you. They're chasing the doxies out, seizing whatever documents they can find, and padlocking the doors. And forget about going to your pet judges and politicians. Any pressure, and I'll start releasing the documents to the Harbor City papers and the local rags. I might anyway, depending on whose names I find and what nasty vices they enjoy. Oh, and I'll tell the papers that you two civic-minded gentlemen gave me the papers voluntarily."

It did not take more than a few seconds before Burke, with Sala a second behind him, asked, "What do you want, Marshal?"

Thorne leaned back in his chair, took a sip of his coffee, and said,

"I want an end to criminals getting rich off weakness and vice. And I want people to start following the laws and commandments the Dear Lord gave us." Thorne sighed, took another sip. "But I'll settle for peace. No more hijackings, no more raids and explosions, no more of anything. Burke, you stay south of the city. Sala, you keep north. If that's too hard for you, then I'll get myself some munitions and blow up all of your roadhouses at once. The blasts will be so loud that it will scare the dwayyo and snallygasters right out of these woods. Do you understand me?"

After reluctant yeses from both men, Thorne told his deputies to take them back. Once they were gone, Syn came over to sit with Thorne.

He had questions for the marshal. *How did he know about Costello? Why wasn't he looking for the men who attacked the Lambert? How does he know where to get munitions, and had he already done so?*

But these were questions for a lawman to ask a suspect. And Syn didn't think he had enough cause to consider the marshal one, not officially that is.

Instead, Syn said, "It's a start."

"Not much of one," Thorne replied. "A month or two, and it will start again. Well, they were warned." Then as if to himself, the marshal said, "At least they won't be suspecting ..."

"Suspecting what?" Syn asked.

Thorne answered quickly. "Won't be suspecting each other of plotting against each other."

The Scarecrow did not believe the smile that accompanied Thorne's answer.

"Well," he said, standing up, "I've got a few crimes to solve," he told Thorne.

He left Thorne to finish the rest of his coffee. As he walked out to his pickup, Syn said to himself, *And later tonight, a person to follow.*

Theodore Syn's tour of duty ended on a good note. The nighttime house break-ins over in Holden turned the work of a disturbed teen who thrilled to the idea of creeping around a house when its occupants were asleep. The young man also liked money and was caught when he tried to hock an easily identifiable watch. Gently questioning him, Syn got him to confess to the whole string. He then called in a favor to get the teen the help he'd need with his problem.

Syn also found the man who had robbed the First Dunkirk Bank. That case was so easy to solve he felt guilty taking his pay for the time he spent on it.

"If you're going to follow in the footsteps of Dutch Anderson and Big John Ashely," he told the robber, "don't borrow your neighbor's car for your getaway."

After his shift, Syn went to his boarding house, talked Mrs. Taylor into an early dinner, then drove back to the Marshal's office. He parked two blocks away and waited to see if Thorne would leave.

I'll give him an hour past sunset, maybe a little more. As he waited, he again heard the whistling cry of the snallygaster.

As he thought, *Good hunting, cousin,* he felt a mental shiver, as if he had received a reply.

The Moon rose, its reflected light shining over all. Thorne left shortly after. As he pulled away, Syn followed, careful not to get too close.

Thorne pulled on to the Coast City Pike. Bixby then, the scarecrow decided and dropped back just a bit. Spot check, maybe? Or something else. Maybe something Burke would not suspect. Syn would know once he got there.

"Sean."

Jack turned toward the whisper in the shadow. "What is it?"

"Tonight's the night. Gather the dwayyo. Have them attack the Holden House."

"So soon?"

"Paddy doesn't want to wait. Do you want one of these?"

The man in the shadows stepped into the light just enough so that Jack could see the Thompson machine gun in his hand. Duffy had let Jack fire his once. It kicked in his hands. He lost control of the weapon, shot up some trees, and killed three birds and a squirrel.

"No, thanks. I'll stick with this." He held up his shotgun.

"Take plenty of shells then."

Jack didn't feel right leaving his post, but that's what the man said Burke wanted him to do. As he walked around to the front, he wondered why Burke had offered the Thompson. He'd been watching when Jack had shot up the trees. Maybe it was the idea of the nameless guy who passed on Jack's secret messages.

He slipped into the dark woods, seen only by two men.

Russell Thorne watched as his dupe went into the woods. *Tonight,* he thought, *tonight the cleansing begins.*

Syn watched as Thorne emerged from the shadows. He had been talking to Jack Reilly, the one some people had started calling the Shotgun Kid. The name was mostly from his carrying the gun around almost every place he went, although there were some rumors that Jack had used it once or twice to carry out Burke's wishes.

Was he one of Thorne's informants? Syn wondered. *No, a man like Reilly was loyal to only one master.*

Syn was about to step forward to confront Thorne when he saw Reilly running away from the roadhouse. He was running toward the woods where moving shadows awaited him.

Some say that faith is the belief in the truth of things for which there is no proof. An epiphany is a sudden realization of that truth. That moment came for Theodore Syn when he saw Jack Reilly enter the woods to be greeted by shadows that would mean death for any other man and Syn knew, without any proof, that things were about to go Hell and that there was nothing he could do about it.

It is time, Jack thought toward the members of the pack that had met him. There were four of them, three almost as tall as a man, the other much taller. *Where are the others?*

There are no others, sent Annarr, *we are all that is needed.*

Then follow me and I will lead you...

NO! the voice from the one who "spoke" with him was a mental shout that almost caused Jack to pass out. *We follow only our pack leader, and he tells us that tonight we hunt men.* She looked toward the Bixby House. *We will begin with those below.*

No! Jack thought back with as much force as he could. *They are MY pack. The ones I will lea...take you to are the ones who mean harm to your pack and mine.*

Very well, we will go with you, sent the group leader. Then to herself, she added, *And on another night we will come back for the others. All the others.*

"What are you doing here, Scarecrow?"

"I was about to ask you the same question, Russ." Looking into the woods, Syn watched as the shadows faded, Reilly having become one of them. "You've been using Reilly, haven't you?"

"Boy's name isn't Jack Reilly. He's a runaway from Baltimore by the name of Sean Meadows. He used to live here. He ran back home and got in with Burke. Here's a tip, Scarecrow, if you're gonna run away, don't run to someplace where so many people know you."

"What about his family?"

Thorne shrugged then pointed toward the woods. "I think he's found a new one. For as long as they last at least."

"The bombing, the Lambert massacre, it's been you all the time, hasn't it? And now you're gonna use Reilly to cause the dwayyo to attack...what?"

"The Holden House, for a start," Thorne admitted. "*The beasts of the Abyss will descend upon the sinners and destroy them. Then, in turn, they will be destroyed themselves.* Scarecrow, I plan to wipe out all the evil in this county — the beasts, the criminals, even Satan's great dragons. Once people learn of how beasts with an appetite for human flesh attacked the roadhouses, they will rise up and hunt them to extinction. The dwayyo, then snallygasters, the purveyors of sin and vice. Only then will there be the Lord's Peace."

Taking an all-too-familiar stance, Theodore Syn said, "Can't let you do that, Russ."

"You have no choice. It's all in motion, you can't stop it."

"I have to try."

Thorne made his move. Syn made his faster. Before the marshal could draw his gun, Syn hit him with the barrel of his, knocking him out.

After tying up the unconscious man who had once been his friend and throwing him into the back of his truck, Syn knew what he had to do. He also knew that he would probably be too late. Praying that he had enough of Jeremiah Syn's blood in him, he set out for the high ground.

It should have been an easy run, but the one who called himself "Jack," the one Verr had told her would guide, did not know the ways of the dark wood. Too many times, the group had to slow to a walk to allow him to catch up with them.

When this is done, he will leave his pack, and it will be stronger for it, Annarr decided. Then a forbidden thought. *Why is our leader doing this? Where is he leading us, and is he leading wisely? Perhaps he is getting old.* Annarr thought of Naester, who had argued against this raid. *He is wise but not strong enough to lead.* Then in her mind, Annarr saw herself running at the front of the pack, taking the choicest meats, and choosing the strongest males when the time came. She thought of this and decided that it was good.

After much too long a time, Jack said they had completed their run. Stopping at the edge of the woods, standing in the shadow of the Moon, they looked down on the place where the men gathered.

We wait until a large crowd goes in, Jack sent to them. *The door will be open, and we can rush in.*

Annarr did not know what a door was but saw it in his mind and so understood. It was protection for this den. She thought this a good idea.

We will rush in, she replied. *You will go last and use your thunder to stop the prey from escaping.*

The man Jack nodded, his mind signaling agreement while his scent signaled the excitement they were all feeling, that of a hunter about to take its prey.

NOW, the man Jack sent and as one the four pack members, *her* pack as Annarr had begun to consider them, rushed forward into open ground.

There were smaller roads off the Coast City Pike that ran on either side of the place where the snallygasters dwelt. Syn took one as far as he could, then he turned onto a dirt road, more of a wide path that had been used by 'shiners in the days before the sky beasts had come and this part of the woods was abandoned by them. The roads were overgrown, and Syn knew that even if he succeeded in what he was trying to do, he'd likely be walking back because his truck was not likely to last the journey.

I'll be lucky if it lasts another ten minutes, Syn thought, expecting a tire to go at any time.

Surprisingly, his truck held up. It was a fallen tree that lay across the path that stopped him. Getting out of the cab, he looked to see how much further he had to go.

"Not as close as I'd hoped, closer than I feared," he said aloud. Then, before he set out, he stopped, leaned against his truck, closed his eyes, and calmed his mind.

Cousins, I am coming. I come carrying the essence of one who strengthened your blood. I come with trouble. I come for help.

He waited for a minute or two. The reply, if that what it was and not wishful thinking, was merely a feeling of…amusement mixed with curiosity.

With hope in his heart, his revolver on his belt, and a shotgun in his hand, Theodore Syn began to climb, hoping that he would not end his days as a snack for a snallygaster.

Syn was halfway up when a shadow passed over him. Looking up, he saw a snallygaster circling overhead.

Cousin?

Human.

Well, that tells me where I stand. At least he didn't swoop down and eat me.

Your meat is not to my taste. But my mate likes all blood. You may proceed if you wish.

Chapter Twelve

Mary Elizabeth Stout, along with her husband and another couple, had come to the Holden House from Harbor City "for a bit of fun." As the doorman bid them welcome and hoped that they would have an enjoyable evening, she heard something behind her, something that sounded like...growling. Turning around, she saw four beasts that surpassed her worst nightmare come toward them. If, at that moment, she had run away from the Holden, away from her friends, and away from her husband, she might have survived to tell the story of that terrible night. Instead, she instinctively sought shelter inside, pushing her way through those in the doorway.

It was her frantic appearance and screaming that alerted those inside the roadhouse of the attack. The doorman, wondering what had upset the woman, turned just seconds after she started screaming. He, too, saw the two-legged creatures coming for him. Knowing them for what they were, he tried to run but by this time the dwayyo were upon him. One grabbed him by the neck, its sharp claws opening an artery. As his blood spurted out, he was the first to die.

With Annarr at the head of her small pack, the other three burst into the main room of the Holden. Never before had they seen so many prey at once, and for a moment, they marveled at the bounty. Then, as their minds sent out thoughts to slow and confuse their victims, they began to lay about, killing with tooth and claw, knowing that they would feast well, that there would be no need to share their kills that night.

Shots were fired by the guards stationed inside. But firing accurately in the midst of a panicked crowd is difficult. Their shots killed at least two patrons, mercifully sparing them from a more horrible death. One dwayyo was struck in the shoulder. The wound was not serious, and the shooter quickly learned that shooting but not killing a dwayyo only made them fiercer.

Some tried to escape through the kitchen door. The cooking staff made it, but as for the rest, the dwayyo had been hunters for many centuries and knew how to encircle their prey so that none but a lucky few would escape.

Still others braved the front door, managing to get behind the bear-sized beast closest to it. Just when they believed themselves safe, as they were thanking God for their deliverance from Hell, there was laughter and the roar of thunder as Jack Reilly gleefully shot them down.

The casino off the main room became the last stand for those who survived the initial attack. The room had no exit to the outside, but it would, for a time, be a place of refuge. The door to the main room was shut and locked against both the beasts and the people who desperately pounded on it as they sought safety.

Some inside the casino tried to move the gaming tables against the door. This was not possible as the tables were bolted to the floor to prevent their being moved should trouble break out. Instead, those that were armed took up firing positions behind the tables.

The screaming from the main room lessened, and soon all that could be heard were piteous cries and moans mixed with howling.

"Maybe they're gone," said a woman who had forced herself to the rear of those standing against the back wall in the hopes that she'd be the last to be attacked. As she said this, the casino door splintered as a calf-sized dwayyo broke in. The men with guns fired, and the dwayyo was hit once, twice, a third time, the last shot entering its eye, causing the dwayyo to leave the pack.

As it fell, the men who had killed it gave out a shout. The things could be killed. But their victory was cut short when a shotgun blast took off the head of one and opened the chest of another. Stunned at the sight of the grinning traitor who had joined with the enemy, the others in the casino were easy prey for the remaining dwayyo.

Then it was quiet. Annarr briefly mourned the one who had left her pack then told the remaining two, *Eat your fill.*

As they did, Jack went from body to body with his shotgun, making sure there were no survivors.

Annarr, who now saw herself as a leader, sent her thoughts to the pack, which had followed behind them and waited to see what would happen.

The prey is down, come feast.

As had his great-grandfather before him, Theodore Syn stood before the snallygasters, the great sky beasts about which his great-grandmother had written. Her words had not done them justice. As Syn stood in front of them, their feathers bright even in the moonlight, they were several feet taller than him. Forra, the male, had razor-sharp teeth, fit for rending and tearing flesh. The tentacles of Kona, the female, waved in front of him as if they were antennae sensing his nature. He stood before them for what seemed like forever, but for what was probably only a few minutes.

I sense our blood in you, however faint it is, Kona finally sent to him. *Why have you come?*

Syn was not sure if the snallygasters or even the dwayyo could understand the concept of evil. It did not, after all, exist in their world, only the cruel reality of survival. So he took a moment before he sent back,

There is a man who wishes to destroy those he thinks are his enemy. He had killed many of his kind and now uses the...hairy ones to kill more.

And what is that to us? Forra asked.

Once the hairy ones have done his killing for him, he will get other men to hunt them down because of this killing.

The thoughts that then came into Syn's minds could only be described as laughter.

The hairy ones are great hunters. They do not fear humans, said Forra.

They should, Syn replied. *For once humans decide that a creature is not fit to live, they will put aside all else to destroy it. They will hunt day and night, as the sun shines and as the moon shines. They will find the dens of the hairy ones and, with great weapons, kill the males, females, and cubs until none are left.*

As my mate asked, what is that to us? Without the hairy ones, there is more prey for us.

Oh, great sky beasts, what makes you think they will stop with the hairy ones?

To illustrate his point, knowing he was taking a great risk, Syn called to mind his memories of the Great War, of men killing men in horrible ways, of gas attacks, of cannon fire and its destruction, and, finally, of biplanes fighting in the sky overhead.

The snallygaster understood. Their thoughts were full of fear as they both sent back, *They can fly. They can attack us from the sky. They can destroy us in the air.*

Then, her wings spread in anger, her tentacles seeking something to seize and crush, Kona asked, *Why should we not destroy...*she took the word from Syn's mind...*this evil called humans?*

Again, Syn sent images of war. *Because,* he sent, *you will not survive us. You cannot survive us. The sky beasts will fly no more, the hairy ones will hunt no more, and the world will be a poorer place without the beauty of your flight and the terror of their hunt.*

There was quiet in Syn's mind as he stood there wondering if he would be the first of many humans to be killed by this pair and any other snallygasters they summoned. Would the male rip him to pieces? Would the female envelop him in her tentacles and drain his blood? Had he doomed every human in the area and, in doing so, doomed the great flying beasts?

Judgment came quickly.

We sense the truth of your thoughts, Kona sent. *We wish to help you, not because of our love for your kind but because of our great fear of it.*

Then will you fly to stop the hairy ones?

Forra answered. *We cannot. One of us alone is not enough to stop them. If the two of us went, there would be none left to guard the nest.*

Oh, great sky beasts, if you are willing, if you feel that you can trust me, I will guard your young, protecting them with my life.

You would do this? Kona asked.

Why not? We are, after all, related.

On Jack's advice, the dwayyo dragged the bodies of the ones who had fallen outside into the building. He then turned most of the lights off, giving the Holden House the appearance of being closed, despite there being several hours before the usual closing time and before the pack had to again fade back into the woods.

The human has served his purpose, Verr sent to Annarr. *We need him no longer.*

I thought that at first, but he fought well, she replied. *He defended our pack and killed those who killed Seger.*

He defended our pack against his own kind. Why? For what purpose? Can he be trusted not to turn against us?

He is but one, the pack are many. As long as he is useful, I say he lives.

The hair on Verr's back stiffened and came up. He growled low in his throat.

You say? he sent. *I am pack leader. I say what will and will not be done.*

If Verr expected Annarr to submit, he was wrong. She did not back away, she did not bow down.

Annarr's eyes challenged Verr as she sent, *A wise leader listens to his second. A strong leader does not fear advice.*

Verr was a wise leader. He knew that there was a time for everything, and this was not a time for a challenge. Later he would deal with his second, but not then. Instead, he sent,

And what else do you say, Annarr?

I say that the pack has eaten well tonight on my, on our kill. We should return to the packhome, taking some of the prey with us to feed on later. On another night, we can attack again.

I say, Annarr, that when they see what we have done, the men will hunt us. Let us go to them now. I will lead some of those who did not hunt tonight against Jack's packhome. Naester will lead the rest against another of man's dens. We will slaughter them, feed on them, and make them fear us. You will return to the packhome, taking only the body of the one who left us, Seger, the one you lost. Take the man as well. I will decide his fate later. Naester and I will bring back food for the pack to feed on later. What now do you say?

I say, Pack Leader, that you had best run straight and quick if you wish to do this while the Moon still shines.

Syn watched as Forra and Kona extended their great wings and took flight. Once in the air, they circled each other, and he felt their joy of being in the air together.

Probably the first time since she laid her eggs, he thought. When they get back, I'll probably have to babysit a little longer.

As the pair flew off, he turned toward the nest.

In her diary, Sun's great-grandmother had written of a cave. Forra and Kona's nest was in the open, the back of it against a high outcropping of rock.

Good defensive position, he thought. *Only one way for predators such as the dwayyo to approach, plus an easy escape into the sky if needed.*

He came close and looked at the chicks. They were small copies of their parents, two males, and two females. Near-fledglings, they were almost ready to fly. "All babies are cute," he remembered someone saying, and since these were babies, Syn supposed that applied to them. But it was a terrifying cuteness when he thought of what they would grow to be.

They had not yet noticed that their parents were gone. Instead, they played, as all young ones do. They nipped, clawed, and scratched at each other, not inflicting injury but definitely establishing dominance. The females seemed to be getting the better of the males, wrapping their tiny tentacles around their brothers, the males unable to break their sisters' holds.

The way of life, Syn thought, as he remembered one or two lost loves. *Once they get their arms around you, they never let you go, even if they are a thousand miles or an ocean away.*

Suddenly, one of the female chicks turned and looked at him. He was not their mother or father; this was a stranger. She let out a low whistle, alerting the others. Soon all four were crying for their parents. One of the braver ones stretched his wings as he struggled to get out of his nest. He would defend his siblings, he would protect his nest.

Syn sent back thoughts of peace and safety. This seemed to relax them, if only for a moment. *I am family, I am of your flock*, he thought to them. *I am not a danger. Do not eat me.*

He stepped away, his arms at his sides as if they were folded wings that presented no threat. The brave one settled down, and this calmed the others. Within minutes, as all young ones do, they went back to ignoring him and returned to their playing.

The chicks, we have to go back.

Like Kona, Forra felt the chicks' call for help, felt her motherly panic. Then, she relaxed.

No, all is right. The one who calls himself Scarecrow has calmed them.

They continued across the sky to where the humans dwelt, their minds searching for the hairy ones.

Three groups, Forra sent to his mate.

Yes, but one is returning to their den, the others are in the woods, going left and right to the rising sun.

Even knowing what they must do, they hesitated to do it.

We must part, Kona sent.

If we are to stop them, yes, we must. Their leader goes right, I will follow him.

Then I will go left. Be careful, Forra.

You as well, Kona.

Feelings of love, concern, and farewell passed between the two. Then they swerved off from each other, each toward a battle they did not seek but which had to be fought if their chicks and the chicks after them were to dance in the sky when the moon shone.

Annarr and her pack were halfway to the packhome when one shadow then another passed above them.

The flying ones, pointed out a packmate, *both of them.*

Annarr realized that the nest of the flying ones was unprotected. *Wait,* she ordered. To Jack and the one carrying Seger she sent, *Continue to the packhome.* To the other, *We go to the high ground.*

But Verr has told us…

She cuffed him. *Verr is not here to say. I say we go to the high ground. We will take and eat the flying ones' brood. We will grow strong in mind and body.* Strong enough to defeat Verr and become pack leader. *Come,* she ordered. She growled and bared her teeth. *Unless you are a pup who needs a lesson…*

The cowed dwayyo backed away, lowering its head. *I will come.*

Let us go then.

They were not silent as they traveled through the forest. There was no need. The lesser beasts feared them. The flying ones were behind them. That night, speed was more important than stealth. Soon, they climbed the high ground.

Sooooo-

The Blair House was closing for the night. Unaware of the slaughter at the Holden House, the patrons, most of them from Harbor City, but some from as far as Baltimore, had enjoyed an evening of dancing, dining, drinking, and gambling. Time was called. Last drinks were finished, final bets were made. The losers bemoaned their losses; the winners pocketed their gains.

Guards stationed themselves outside, watching the road for raiders. They were aware of what had happened at the Lambert House and did not want that repeated at the Blair.

The same was occurring at the Bixby House. Happy people, last drinks, last bets, winners and losers. Guards were there as well, watching for trouble, hoping it would not come. Some noted that Jack Reilly was missing, that he had not been seen all night. They thought nothing of it. They didn't like him all that much anyway.

As one, the dwayyo charged both groups. There was screaming as they emerged from the woods, their growls frightening, their minds sending confusing and slowing thoughts. Though the pack had eaten well that night, those attacking intended to get fat on the flesh of man.

Then, at the Blair House, and also at the Bixby, cries came from above, and shadows covered the ground as the snallygasters dropped toward their foes.

Kona's attack at first confused the dwayyo, breaking their concentration and allowing their would-be victims to escape, either running away from the Blair House or taking shelter inside it. The ones who ran became easy prey for the faster beasts, or so the dwayyo thought. Protecting the humans being her first priority, Kona swooped down, grabbed two of the pursuers. She flew high, then dropped them on their pack mates. This scattered all but the ones trying to break down the door of the Blair. The door was thick, but soon wood cracked, and hinges broke. The door fell open. But then Krona again swooped and flew high. Two more dwayyo fell from the sky even as two of them came through the now open door, intent on slaughter.

But this was not the Holden House. Those within the Blair had had time to prepare a defense. When the dwayyo charged inside, they were met by shotgun blasts, pistol shots, and the staccato of a Tommy gun.

A noise from the back, the kitchen door being forced. Two of the guards rushed in only to see blood spurting from a cook's neck. He fired his gun, its slug striking the dwayyo in the shoulder. Bleeding and enraged, it charged the man, gutting him with its claws. Then it ran into the main room where it killed another man and a woman before it was brought down.

Feeling too many of his group leave the pack, sensing that the attack Verr had ordered was a failure, Naester ordered what few remained to withdrawal, but not before Kona took another into the sky. But as she rose, in her mind, she heard the panic of her young. This distracted her enough that the hairy one in her grasp was able to claw her underside, causing her to drop it. It fell, but although its arm was broken, it was able to escape with its pack.

On sensing her young ones' distress, Kona rose high and flew straight toward the nest.

At first, Forra's attack on the dwayyo was much the same as his mate. He swooped in, grabbed two of the hairy ones, flew high, and dropped them. But this was just to scatter them and allow the humans to get to safety. He had another goal in mind.

More interested in stopping the dwayyo than he was in protecting the humans, Forra ignored the pack's assault on them. Instead, his mind sought out Verr's. Finding it, he again swooped down and grabbed the pack leader from behind so that he could not use his claws. Rising into the sky, he sent to Verr,

You fool, you newborn pup. You have been led down the wrong path by the human Jack.

As Forra sent this, Verr twisted his body and turned his head, trying to sink either teeth or claws into the snallygaster.

If you hurt me, Forra sent, *I will drop you, and you will leave the pack, leave it without a leader. If you listen, I will not harm you, not this night anyway.*

Seeing the sense in this, Verr stopped struggling. *How have I been fooled?*

Forra then sent into Verr's mind all that the Scarecrow had told him. About the trap set by Jack and his pack leader, a trap to incite the humans to destroy those of the den and nest. How the humans would seek their destruction. Finally, he sent the dwayyo leader the images of war that the Scarecrow had shared with him.

If they do this to their own kind, what will they do to ours?

Searching Forra's mind, Verr saw the truth in it. *Very well, put me down.* Even before he was on the ground, Verr sent the pack the order to return to the packhome, making sure to take with them the bodies of those who had left the pack.

Forra left Verr in a small clearing just inside the woods.

This changes nothing between us, Flying One, Verr sent.

It changes everything for all of us, Forra replied, *for, after tonight, the humans cannot ignore us.*

As Verr ran off to join his pack, Forra received the message from his mate.

The chicks are in trouble.

He sent back, *I am done here. Let us fly fast.*

A sound in the distance, much like a freight train whistle, told Theodore Syn that Forra and Kona had begun their attack. He looked toward the near-fledglings and said a prayer that their parents would survive the night. Selfishly, he hoped at least one of them returned, for he knew nothing about the chicks left in his care and knew of no one who did.

The young ones stirred. Even at this distance, they could tell that their parents were in danger. If he knew how, Syn would have comforted them.

Then he heard noises on the hill. At first, he thought that Russell Thorne had slipped his bonds, climbed out of the pickup, and was coming after him. Or at least ascending the hill to see where he had been left.

Growls told Syn that he was wrong. Dwayyo, he thought. Sensing danger, the young ones fully awoke and began to cry out. Syn, his senses heightened, felt satisfaction and a killing lust come from the hill.

Two of them, and I'm probably not fast enough to account for one of them. He knew that there were men who, in his situation, would run away, telling themselves there was nothing that they could do and hoping that the dwayyo would be satisfied with the chicks. But the Scarecrow was not that type of man. He had given his word, and whatever the cost, he would keep it.

A plan formed, a dangerous one, one that required him to use his "family" as bait. He ran into the trees closest to the nest, hoping that the panicked thoughts of the infant snallygasters would cover his.

Annarr heard the cries of the infants in her mind. She felt their fear and was pleased. There was something else, something that should not be there, but she did not pay attention to it, knowing that none but the flying ones would be at the nest. With the scent of the helpless prey filling their nostrils, she and her pack member charged.

There came the sound of thunder as her companion was thrown backward. As she felt him leave the pack, she looked toward the nest to see…a man, a man protecting the chicks of the flying ones. *This is what I felt, this is what cannot be.* Enraged, she forgot her young prey and charged the man.

Syn had shot the first dwayyo, the smaller one, the one nearest him, from hiding. Then he stood, distracting the larger one from the hatchlings and focusing its attention on him.

Damn, it's fast, he thought as the growling, maddened beast rushed toward him. It took all he had to wait until it was close enough so that he could not miss. When he saw the redness of its eyes, when he smelled its fetid breath, he fired.

He turned just as the still-moving body of the headless dwayyo struck him. Had he not, he would have been trapped beneath its dead body. Still, he was knocked to the ground. Getting up quickly, he readied himself in case there were others. To his relief, none came.

Letting out a long sigh, Syn offered up prayers of thanks to the Lord and St. Gabriel Possenti, patron of gunmen. Then he checked on the first dwayyo he had shot. It looked dead, but to be sure, he fired another shotgun blast at its head. Looking toward his charges, he saw and felt their excitement. Their fear gone, replaced by…hunger.

"The things you do for family," he said to them. Then, remembering that he had seen bones in their nest, he said, "What are you waiting for? Dinner's on me tonight."

One by one, the young snallygasters left their nest and began to feed.

Forra and Kona were close to the nest. The frantic cries of the young ones had ceased and had been replaced with thoughts of contentment. When they landed, they were surprised to find their hatchlings feeding on the two dead dwayyo.

You have done well, Cousin, Forrra sent to Syn, using the name Scarecrow had given them.

Yes, added Kona. *You have protected the nest and fed the young ones. You are now one of our flock. And once I have recovered from the injury given me by a hairy one...*Forra went over to her and began to fuss. *It is deep but will heal,* she assured him. Once he was convinced she was in no danger, Kona went on. *You are one of our flock, and I would like to add your essence to our line to strengthen it. If you are willing?*

It was the strangest proposition Syn had ever received. Had he not read his great-grandmother's diary, he would not have known what was being asked or how to answer.

I would be honored to fly with you, Cousin Kona, when you are healed. Syn turned toward Forra. *If it is permitted.*

Why would it not be, Cousin Scarecrow?

For this, Syn had no answer, for how could he explain jealousy to one who did not feel it?

There is one other problem, Syn sent.

Yes, answered Forra. *Many humans have died tonight at the teeth and claws of the hairy ones. Many humans have lived to tell the tale. The pack has been diminished and will be hunted and destroyed. Then the humans will turn to us. We, too, were seen, we too will be hunted despite our efforts on man's behalf. Just as the pack must leave, so we must fly and seek another nest.*

Syn thought for a moment. *Maybe not. Are there others of your kind near?*

Forra thought to him of the lone snallygaster of York and of the pair in Frederick. There were some others in the south.

Make them all aware of what has happened. Once they are, on a single night, when the Moon shines, unite in thought, send your own tale across the land, and convince the humans that you are merely the stuff of their dreams and legends. We humans tend not to believe in things we do not understand. Soon, when your shadows cross the light of the Moon, they will think you nothing more than clouds or tricks of the light.

That is wise, Cousin Scarecrow, Kona thought to him. *And we could do that, hiding from the humans in much the same way we hide when we sleep.*

With that, Syn took leave of the snallygaster, for it had been a long night. But before he left, he told them,

The one who started this all, who set human against human, who would have seen both you and the dwayyo ended is at the bottom of the hill. I will leave him for you to deal with as you see fit.

You would give up one of your own kind? Forra asked.

He is not my kind. He is a monster.

We do not know what that is.

Be happy for that, Cousin Kona. Be happy for that.

Two nights after the snallygasters of Corbett County fought with and defeated the dwayyo, they called their cousins from York, Frederick, and beyond to gather at their nest. Never had so many gathered in one place. Together they sent thoughts of themselves to all who could receive them. Slowly and carefully, they removed all knowledge of their existence and that of the dwayyo from the minds of humankind.

With the dwayyo having fled and the snallygasters mostly forgotten, the deaths at the Bixby, the Holden, and the Blair were attributed to gang violence. So many died that the newspapers and the public demanded that something be done.

With an investigation by the State Police pending, one day, men sent by the crime lords of Harbor City came for Vincent Sala and Patrick Burke. The two were driven away and were never seen again.

The Treasury Department closed all the roadhouses, but they did not stay closed. People will have their vices.

The dwayyo had been diminished. Too many had left the pack. Some of those who survived blamed the man Jack who had remained with them. Most, however, felt that it was because of Veer's orders.

The night after the attacks on the men, the pack gathered. Naester stepped forth. His hair raised, his claws extended, his teeth bared, he offered Verr challenge.

Knowing his time had passed, Verr accepted, but offered only token resistance. After exchanging a few blows, after receiving a few wounds, he backed away from Naester and submitted, baring his throat for the killing blow. Naester struck with his claw but left only a scratch.

The pack is too few, we will need your strength, the new leader sent to Verr, adding, *and I will need your wisdom.*

Fearful that the men they had for so long hunted would now hunt them, the pack left the woods. When the man Jack followed them, Naester allowed it, telling the pack, *He knows the ways of men. He might be of use.*

Naester led his pack away north, then east around the water, then south. Traveling and hunting by night, they finally ended their journey on an island near the ocean, finding refuge in the forest close to where the horses swam. Soon, like the snallygasters, they were forgotten by all but a few.

Russell Thorne's blood-drained body was never found. He was believed to have been yet another victim of what the papers were calling the Corbett County Night of Blood.

With Thorne's disappearance, Theodore Syn, called "Scarecrow" by some and "Cousin" by the great sky beasts, was named acting marshal until a new one could be appointed. He stayed in that post for two months until one day he received a call, one he had no choice but to answer. And that night, he willingly danced in the sky with a snallygaster and was forever changed by the experience.

Not all forgot. There were those who had seen and so still believed, or whose minds were too strong or different to be changed. Still, the snallygasters, the flying ones, the Great Sky Beasts soon passed into myth and legend, unknown to most and only seen by those wise enough to believe and lucky enough to be looking up as their shadows crossed the shining Moon.

ABOUT THE AUTHOR

JOHN L. FRENCH is a retired crime scene supervisor with forty years' experience. He has seen more than his share of murders, shootings, and serious assaults. As a break from the realities of his job, he started writing science fiction, pulp, horror, fantasy, and, of course, crime fiction.

John's first story, "Past Sins," was published in Hardboiled Magazine and was cited as one of the best Hardboiled stories of 1993. More crime fiction followed, appearing in Alfred Hitchcock's Mystery Magazine, the Fading Shadows magazines, and in collections by Barnes and Noble. Association with writers like James Chambers and the late, great C.J. Henderson led him to try horror fiction and to a still-growing fascination with zombies and other undead things. His first horror story, "The Right Solution," appeared in Marietta Publishing's *Lin Carter's Anton Zarnak*. Other horror stories followed in anthologies such as *The Dead Walk* and *Dark Furies*, both published by Die Monster Die books. It was in *Dark Furies* that his character Bianca Jones made her literary debut in "21 Doors," a story based on an old Baltimore legend and a creepy game his daughter used to play with her friends.

John's first book was *The Devil of Harbor City*, a novel done in the old pulp style. *Past Sins* and *Here There Be Monsters* followed. John was also a consulting editor for Chelsea House's *Criminal Investigation* series. His other books include *The Assassins' Ball* (written with Patrick Thomas), *Souls on Fire, The Nightmare Strikes, Monsters Among Us, The Last Redhead, the Magic of Simon Tombs*, and *The Santa Heist* (written with Patrick Thomas). John is the editor of *To Hell in a Fast Car, Mermaids 13*, C. J. Henderson's *Challenge of the Unknown, Camelot 13* (with Patrick Thomas), and (with Greg Schauer) *With Great Power*...

You can find John on Facebook, or you can email him at him at jfrenchfam@aol.com.

artist's rendition of a Snallygaster

SNALLYGASTERS

(From the German *Schneller Geist* meaning "quick spirit." Also referred to as a "sky beast" by Native American nations.)

ORIGINS: This cryptid was first sighted in Frederick County at the beginning of the 20th century. It is believed to be a reappearance of creatures encountered by the German immigrants that settled in the Blue Ridge Mountains in the early 18th century who were terrorized by a creature they referred to as *Schneller Geist*, or quick spirit.

Slaves were warned against escape lest they encounter the snallygasters in their flight.

The only known protections against this creature are avoidance, and a seven-pointed star called a hex sign, such as those found on many barns in Pennsylvania Dutch country.

It is said the Dwayyo, another Maryland region cryptid, are their mortal enemies (see following listing).

There are some theories that the snallygaster may be related to similar creatures cited in Native American lore.

DESCRIPTION: Though many eye-witness accounts vary, it is generally agreed that this large flying creature is part avian and part reptile, with wings spanning at least twelve to fourteen feet and stood to a height of up to twenty feet. By comparison, it was estimated to be the size of an dirigible. In some accounts, the snallygaster has a long, needle-like beak, claws and teeth like steel, and a tail twenty feet long. Other features cited are fur instead of feathers, horns, tentacles, and dragon-like aspects. There is some debate whether the snallygaster has monocular or binocular vision. Some theorize that the creature may have had the chameleon-like ability to alter not just its form, but also its size and color. The cries of the snallygaster range from a shrill screech to a blood-curdling roar to a whistle said to be similar to a locomotive. A snallygaster was reported to have killed a man by piercing his neck and sucking his blood. They are also known to carry off both children and cattle.

LIFE CYCLE: The life expectancy of a snallygaster is believed to be no more than twenty years.

artist's rendition of a Dwayyo

There are several accounts of the discovery of nests and eggs, generally on cliff faces at a great height, though early records denote a preference for nesting in caves.

The young are hatched from massive eggs large enough to produce offspring the size of a horse or an elephant. It is not known if the young hatch dependent, as with avian offspring; or self-sufficient, as with reptilian young.

HISTORY: There are some claims that early media coverage was a hoax, but sightings and accounts continued well into the mid-twentieth century.

A resurgence of sightings in Frederick County began in 1909, as cited in Middletown's *Valley Register*, but were not limited to this region. There were accounts of encounters all over Maryland, as well as Ohio, Washington DC, West Virginia, and New Jersey.

Accounts of the snallygaster have also been featured in the *Baltimore Sun*, *National Geographic*, and *Time Magazine*, and in 1976, The Washington Post sponsored a search for the snallygaster and other regional cryptids.

The Smithsonian offered a $100,000 reward for the hide of a snallygaster, and by some accounts, President Theodore Roosevelt considered hunting the beast.

Evidence for the existence of this cryptid was reported in 1932, when the skeletal remains of a snallygaster were found in a mash vat in a moonshine factory in Hagerstown, Maryland. Before these remains could be recovered, revenue agents destroyed the vat with dynamite.

Although no sightings have been reported in recent years, they are still believed to be active in the mountains of western Maryland, especially around Frederick County.

DWAYYO (OR DEWAYO)

ORIGINS: Accounts of this cryptid first appear in Frederick County dating back as early as the 1920's and '30's, but could date back as far as the 1700s, believed by some to be related to the Dutch hexenwolf. German settlers of the region counted the dwayyo as protection against the snallygasters, their natural enemy, thus the paint or hanging of hex signs on buildings in the community to this day. Other accounts cite them as the earliest occurrence of dogmen.

DESCRIPTION: These are bipedal creatures ranging in height from four to eight feet tall or more. There have been reports of them running on all fours, but their general stance is noted as upright. They have canine or wolf-like features and bushy tails and long hair. Their coats can be a range of colors, from black, dark brown, grey, fawn, or brindle, sometimes with stripes on their lower section. Some reports note powerful legs, muscular like a kangaroo. Their cries are most described as horrid screams.

LIFE CYCLE: Little is known about the life expectancy of dwayyo, or the stages of their life. It is known that they are pack animals. They are photophobic and avoid bright light and thus are usually nocturnal hunters.

HISTORY: Though there are early accounts of this creature, the period of greatest activity appears to have been in the 1960s and 70s. The last reported sighting of the dwayyo was in 2009 in the Gambrill State Park in Frederick County, Maryland.

ABOUT THE ARTIST

Although Jason Whitley has worn many creative hats, he is at heart a traditional illustrator and painter. With author James Chambers, Jason collaborates and illustrates the sometimes-prose, sometimes graphic novel, *The Midnight Hour,* which is being collected into one volume by eSpec Books. His and Scott Eckelaert's newspaper comic strip, Sea Urchins, has been collected into four volumes. Along with eSpec Books' Systema Paradoxa series, Jason is working on a crime noir graphic novel. His portrait of Charlotte Hawkins Brown is on display in the Charlotte Hawkins Brown Museum.

CAPTURE THE CRYPTIDS!

Cryptid Crate is a monthly subscription box filled with various cryptozoology and paranormal themed items to wear, display and collect. Expect a carefully curated box filled with creeptastic pieces from indie makers and artisans pertaining to bigfoot, sasquatch, UFOs, ghosts, and other cryptid and mysterious creatures (apparel, decor, media, etc).

http://CryptidCrate.com

CPSIA information can be obtained
at www.ICGtesting.com
Printed in the USA
FSHW010718201020